Once Upon A
Midnight Clear

To: Lyra
Happy Holidays!

Jacqul E Smit

Jacqueline E. Smith

Wind Trail Publishing

Once Upon A Midnight Clear

Wind Trail Publishing
PO Box 830851
Richardson, TX 75083-0851
www.WindTrailPublishing.com

First Paperback Edition, January 2019

ISBN-13: 978-0-9972450-8-0
ISBN-10: 0-9972450-8-5

Cover Design: Wind Trail Publishing
Cover Photograph: Bruno Glätsch

In loving memory of two remarkable women.

Donna Carruth, owner of Joy's Hallmark, my first employer, lifelong friend, and the brightest light our little town has ever known. A true Christmas Queen.

And Gloria Snyder, my elementary school Principal, whose love and kindness helped to shape my childhood. I will always remember her for her gentle beauty and her angelic singing voice.

CHAPTER ONE

Royal Wedding Countdown: Only Three Weeks Left!

Nicolás and Britt: Happily Ever After in the Making!

San Cecilio's Very Own Cinderella Set to Marry Prince Charming on Christmas Day!

Prince Nicolás was never one to believe in fairy tales... until an enchanting young travel writer appeared on the scene. After a chance meeting on the Square and more than a few romantic walks through the castle gardens, the handsome Prince got down on one knee and asked Brittany Walker for her hand. A commoner by birth, the lovely and spirited Miss Walker has adapted to her newfound place in the public eyes with grace and humility.

"She'll be the perfect Princess," a source close to the royal couple claims. "She loves Nicolás and she loves the people of San Cecilio. And by all accounts, the feeling is mutual."

Although the soon-to-be HRH has indeed captured the hearts of her future subjects, certain members of the royal family were not so easily won.

"It has been understood for years that Prince Nicolás would marry Princess Rosalind of Mondovia. Breaking that betrothal was a risky political move for the Principality of San Cecilio. But Nicolás was most insistent. If he couldn't marry Britt, then he wouldn't marry at all."

In the months following her royal engagement, Miss Walker has attended Princess lessons, met with foreign dignitaries, and even accompanied Prince Nicolás to state dinners. In addition, she has immersed herself in the royal charities and has become a goodwill ambassador for numerous causes and organizations.

She may not be of royal blood, but in her heart, Brittany Walker is the very definition of a Princess. And in the end, the heart is all that matters.

"You're doing it again, aren't you?"

Once upon a time, I truly believed that having my own office in my own wing of the palace meant that I would finally have a space all to myself. A sanctuary, if you will. Or if not a sanctuary, then at least a personal retreat which would require one to knock before entering.

I think it goes without saying that that was a dream that did not come true.

"No," I answer automatically, shutting my laptop before my nosy brother can peer over my shoulder.

"You're lying."

"No, I'm not." Princesses never lie. We embellish.

"You know you're not doing anybody any favours by obsessing over those articles," Robert declares, making himself comfortable on my sofa. "If anything, you're only making yourself more miserable."

"Thank you for that, oh fount of all wisdom."

"Come on, Rose. I thought you had gotten past all this."

"I have. But have you seen these headlines? *San Cecilio's Own Cinderella*? She's not one of their own! She's an American! She's from Indiana. Oh, and she's not a travel writer, either. She's a travel *agent* who just happens to have a blog."

"My God, have you any idea how petty you sound?"

"Yes, actually. I am well aware." Just as I'm sure he's aware of how amused *he* sounds. Perhaps I'd be laughing too if I weren't the one San Cecilio's so-called Prince Charming had so unceremoniously rejected.

"I suppose you have every right to be. I know this hasn't been easy for you," Robert sighs, toying with the golden ring on his right hand. "How *are* you doing?"

As a working royal and heir to our father's throne here in Mondovia, Robert rarely finds time to exchange pleasantries or engage in heart-to-heart talks with his sullen little sister, so I appreciate his asking.

"I don't know," I finally answer. In a lot of ways, I think I'm still trying to process everything. After all, my entire life was thrown off course the moment Nicolás announced his intention to marry Miss Walker. My future, which had once been set in stone, was suddenly a blank slate. Others may have found it freeing. Me? I just felt lost. "I think there's a part of me that truly believed that it wouldn't happen. That he wouldn't really go through with it."

"I think we all harboured similar doubts." My brother's eyes are warm and sympathetic. I've always envied him those eyes. He inherited our father's hazel eyes that shine a brilliant green and gold in the sunlight. Our mother and I, on the other hand, share eyes so dark brown that they appear almost black even on the brightest of days.

3

"I suppose I should be grateful," I muse aloud. "It's not like he left me nursing a broken heart."

"You really don't love him?"

"Well, of course I love him. We've known each other our whole lives. But I was never *in* love with him." At least, I don't think I was. Had I fantasized about our life together? Certainly. Had I dreamed of my wedding day? Without a doubt. But looking back, none of those daydreams or fleeting fancies had anything to do with Nicolás himself. They were more about finally taking my place in the world and all of the wonderful things that were supposed to be waiting for me. As special as Nicolás is to me, I've never felt my heart skip a beat when I catch a glimpse of him from across the room or fallen asleep imagining myself in his arms.

Still, that doesn't make it easier to watch the man I was supposed to marry walk down the aisle with someone else.

"Yet you still would have married him?" Robert asks.

"You know I would have." It may not have been my dream to marry Nicolás, but it was my duty. And for the past twenty-seven years, duty is all I've known.

"That's what sets us apart. I'm not so sure I could go through with an arranged marriage."

"You would if it was what was best for your country."

Robert looks like he wants to contradict me, but we both know it's the truth. There are many privileges to being born royal, but personal interest isn't one of them.

4

Knock knock knock.

Neither is privacy.

"Yes, come in!" I call to the person outside of my office.

The door opens slowly and Mrs. Aldridge, my mother's personal secretary steps inside.

"I beg your pardon, Your Royal Highness, but Her Majesty wishes to speak with you."

"Both of us?" Robert asks.

"No, Your Royal Highness. Just Princess Rosalind."

"I'll be right down," I promise. "Thank you, Mrs. Aldridge."

Mrs. Aldridge nods politely before exiting the room.

"Well, I mustn't keep Mother waiting," I announce, closing my computer and rising up to straighten my skirt.

"Wait." Robert stops me. "I know that you know this, but as your brother, I feel I need to say it at least once more."

"Go on."

"You're strong, Rose. You're strong and you're brave. And I want you to remember that next time you're tempted to lock yourself away here in your tower of isolation and self-pity."

"It's my office. I'm supposed to lock myself in here."

"Be that as it may, I don't want to walk in again to find you scowling at your computer screen."

"Then knock." I'm not teasing. I'm absolutely serious. But he laughs nevertheless.

And I suppose that's why I love him.

My mother is already sipping her afternoon tea when I arrive in the sitting room. It's a beautiful space with a soothing atmosphere with burgundy carpet, lush beige sofas, and quaint crystal chandeliers. It's where I go when I want to feel truly at home. I'll settle in with a blanket and a good book or perhaps paint the flowers in the gardens below.

Or, in this instance, enjoy a cup of tea with my mother while she discusses matters which, I'm sure, are of the utmost importance.

"Rosalind, Darling. Come in," she smiles. She's already poured me a cup of tea which generally means she's hoping to get straight to business. Sure enough, I've barely taken a seat in the chair next to her before she says, "I've just spoken with Isabel."

Princess Isabel is Nicolás's mother. Since San Cecilio is a principality, it's ruled by a Prince and Princess rather than a King and Queen.

"Oh? How is she?"

"As one might expect with a wedding in three weeks." That's my mother's polite way of saying that her friend is under an inordinate amount of stress.

"Well, I'm sure she was delighted to hear from you."

"Yes. In fact, she asked if I would be willing to fly down a few weeks early to lend a helping hand and a smiling face. Which, of course I would if my schedule would permit. But you know how overwhelming the holiday season can be."

She doesn't have to explain it to me. The days and weeks leading up to Christmas are the busiest time of year for our family. There are dinners and balls and charity appearances, not to mention the personal visits to our extended family and close friends. I love Christmas and I always have, but I daresay it would be nice to take things slow for once and really savor the season.

"I'm certain she understands," I tell my mother.

"Oh, of course she does. However..."

Oh, no.

I don't know what she's about to say to me, but I can tell by the way she's fiddling with her teaspoon that she knows I won't be happy to hear it.

"I do want her to know that she has our family's full support," she continues. "That's why I was wondering if it wouldn't be a good idea..."

Don't say it.

"... for you to go in my place."

Oh, you said it.

"You want me to go to San Cecilio?"

"Yes."

"To the castle?"

"Yes."

"For three weeks?"

"You'll be so busy, your time will fly by," Mother assures me. "Just think. You'll get to go to banquets and dress fittings and rehearsals..."

"Mother, please know that I say this with the utmost respect, but I can't think of anything I'd rather *not* do."

"Oh, but Darling, don't you see? This is a wonderful opportunity for you to act as an ambassador for Mondovia. Not to mention a chance to show the people of San Cecilio and the rest of the world that the bond between our nations is stronger than ever."

"Yes, that all sounds well and good. But you *know* the press is going to obliterate me the moment I set foot in San Cecilio. They're not going to see a goodwill gesture between nations. They're going to see a jilted bride seeking revenge and trying to sabotage the wedding." Just like they did after Nicolás and Miss Walker first announced their engagement.

"Not if you show up with a smile on your face."

"I could show up wearing a Team Brittany T-shirt and they'd still think I only came to try to win Nicolás back."

"Then let them think it. It doesn't matter. What matters is your love and support for Nicolás. And Miss Walker."

I avert my gaze. I know she's right. And she knows she has me.

"Very well," I sigh. "When do I leave?"

CHAPTER TWO

San Cecilio is a small, landlocked nation on the Iberian Peninsula with a population of just around 85,000. Surrounded by majestic mountains that glow with lush green foliage in the summertime and sparkle with fresh snow in the winter, San Cecilio used to be one of the avid European traveler's best-kept secrets.

Needless to say, everything changed when Prince Nicolás announced his intention to marry an American. Now the once-quiet streets are constantly bustling with starry-eyed foreigners hoping to find their own happily-ever-after. In a lot of ways, the thriving tourism industry has been wonderful for San Cecilio and especially its capital city, Valoña. But I also know that its residents miss their days of peace and simplicity.

Due to aforementioned vacationers, it takes the royal motorcade nearly two hours to reach the castle; a journey that used to take a mere thirty minutes. Fortunately, the world outside my window is beautiful. And I have my lady-in-waiting, Sophie, to keep me company.

Standing amidst a grove frost-covered trees and blanketed by a layer of snow, the castle itself is a vision of winter magic. Although slightly smaller than our palace back home, it's always reminded me of a castle you'd see in a storybook with its stone walls and lofty turrets.

Passing the familiar castle guards, Sophie and I finally step through the castle doors and into the grand foyer, where Felipe, the royal family's gatekeeper, greets us with a bow and a fond grin.

"*Bienvenidos, Princesa.* I trust you had a pleasant flight?" he asks.

"It was lovely. Thank you, Felipe," I reply.

"Rosalind!" A new voice echoes across the hall.

I turn to see my lifelong friend and former intended, His Royal Highness Prince Nicolás. He's as charming and polished as ever in his typical designer suit but there's something... different about him. His dark hair is a little longer than I remember, his smile a little brighter. But it's in his eyes, those captivating gray eyes, that I see the true transformation. His eyes, once so stern and serious, are now alight with joy and wonder. And love. So much love.

"Hello, my friend," he says, welcoming me with a warm embrace.

"Nicolás." I can't help but smile. "You look wonderful."

"I feel wonderful. And I am so glad you're here. And Sophie, welcome."

"Thank you, Your Highness." Sophie curtsies.

"Come. Follow me!" Nicolás says, taking my hand and guiding me toward the corridor. "I want you to meet Brittany."

"Oh... now?" I had hoped I might get the chance to freshen up, perhaps even shower, before being formally introduced to Miss Walker.

"*Sí.* She's very excited to meet you. And of course, my mother is waiting to welcome you, too."

He leads me to the castle library, where an elegant dark-haired woman sits by the fire sorting through a chest of Christmas ornaments while a petite blonde girl dressed in an oversized jumper, leggings, and boots hangs a glittering poinsettia on the tree in the center of the room.

"Look who finally showed up!" Nicolás announces.

"Rosalind! Oh, my dear! It is so wonderful to see you!" Princess Isabel exclaims, rising to greet me.

"You as well, Your Highness. Thank you for having me." I adore Princess Isabel. For as long as I can remember, she's been a second mother to me. She's kind, she's compassionate, and she's the sort of person who makes everyone around her feel at home.

"Oh, the pleasure is ours."

"Rosalind! Finally!" The blonde girl in boots approaches with an eager wave and smiles at me as though we've known each other all our lives. "It's so nice to meet you! I'm Brittany!"

And then this girl who is, in fact, a perfect stranger, throws her arms around me, all but knocking the air clear out of my lungs. I'm so startled that I take an involuntary step back, nearly colliding with Nicolás.

"Whoa! Careful!" he laughs.

"I'm sorry. Did I do something wrong?" Brittany asks.

"No, no. Not at all, Miss Walker," I assure her. "Forgive me, I'm not accustomed to so much... enthusiasm."

"I know I'm supposed to curtsy and all that, but Nick has told me so many nice things about you I feel like we're practically family!"

"...Nick?" I must not have heard her correctly.

11

"That's what Britt calls me," Nicolás explains, blushing all the way to his ears.

"Oh how... charming." I'll admit, I've never been one for nicknames or abbreviations. True, Robert calls me Rose, but he's my brother. He's permitted.

"Rosalind, is there anything we can get you? Water? Tea? I have some fresh Christmas cookies baking in the kitchen," Brittany smiles.

"Thank you, but I was actually wondering if I might rinse off in the shower before settling in."

"Of course, my dear. You do whatever you need, and join us again when you're ready," Isabel says. "We'll be decorating all afternoon."

"And then, after dinner, we're having a movie night!" Brittany announces. "We're going to change into our pajamas, make popcorn, spread out a dozen blankets in front of the fire, and watch Christmas movies. You're welcome to join us!"

"We might even have a surprise for you," Nicolás adds.

"For me?" I ask. "What is it?"

"If we told you, it wouldn't be a surprise."

This is strange. The Nicolás I know doesn't do surprises. Neither do I, if I'm being perfectly honest. I think it's fair to say I'm feeling a little apprehensive. I try not to let it show, however, as Felipe arrives to escort me to my bedroom.

"It is such a delight to have you here with us, *Princesa*," he says. "Especially considering the... special circumstances."

I don't have to ask what he means, but I do wish he hadn't said it. I'm happy to know that there are those out there who don't view me as the villain of Nicolás and Brittany's story. Now if only they wouldn't cast me as the victim.

"Thank you, Felipe. I'm happy to be here."

"It is going to be a wonderful holiday. You'll see."

I nod politely, hoping with all I have in me that he's right.

Finally, we arrive at my bedroom, where Sophie has already unpacked my belongings and laid out a new outfit for tonight. She rises up out of her chair as soon as I walk in. Not out of respect, mind you. She wants to hear all about Nicolás's new bride-to-be.

"Well?" she asks. "Did you meet her?"

"I did."

"And?"

Let it be known that a Princess never engages in gossip. Unless she's with her lady-in-waiting.

"She's... very friendly."

"Oh?"

"She hugged me."

"Oh."

"But she seems to be a very good person. And Nicolás... well, I've never seen him so happy," I tell her. "She was wearing *leggings* though. In the presence of Princess Isabel."

"You're joking."

"And boots."

"You mean...?"

"Like the kind you see on teenagers in television shows."

"And Her Royal Highness... was okay with this?"

"She didn't seem to mind at all."

"Fascinating."

"Then Miss Walker invited me to a movie night."

"Oh. That was nice of her. Are you going to go?"

"I don't know. Nicolás said they had a *surprise* for me."

"What sort of surprise?"

"I'm almost afraid to find out."

"Maybe it's an early Christmas present. Like a new scarf. Or leggings," Sophie giggles.

"Very funny," I cast her a sidelong glance before gathering up my clothes and retreating to the bathroom for a well-deserved and long overdue shower.

By the time I arrive back in the library, the Christmas tree is almost fully decorated and a plate of fresh gingerbread cookies sits waiting on the desk in the corner of the room.

"*Perfecto*! You're just in time!" Nicolás exclaims.

"Just in time for what?" I ask.

"Your surprise has arrived."

"Oh?" I glance around the library. I don't see a surprise.

"Stay here. I'll go fetch it," Nicolás grins before darting out of the room, leaving me alone with his mother and Brittany.

"Should I be nervous?" I ask Princess Isabel.

"Not at all!" Brittany answers for her. "You're going to love it! And you look absolutely gorgeous."

14

"Why, thank you." It's an unexpected, though not unwelcome compliment. "You look lovely as well."

As far as appearances go, Brittany and I could not be more dissimilar. Whereas she is fair and delicate, almost elfin in appearance, I am tall, brunette, and shapely. And although I have been raised to never equate physical beauty with self-worth, standing next to Brittany, I suddenly find myself feeling terribly inadequate.

Before I'm able to dwell on this new sense of insecurity, the door opens and Nicolás reappears, still smiling as broadly as before. Only now, he's not alone. He's accompanied by a young man with impeccably styled light-brown hair, blue eyes, and a confident smile. He's dressed in a tan suit and around his wrist glistens a golden watch that must have cost more than a small fortune.

"Your Highnesses," Nicolás announces. "May I present Lord Weston Bentley."

"Ah, yes. Lord Weston, welcome," Princess Isabel smiles.

"Thank you, Your Royal Highness." The young man bows. "And may I just say what a privilege it is to be invited to share the holiday season with you."

"Think nothing of it. We are delighted to have you."

"So delighted!" Brittany exclaims, running to embrace Weston. "Thank you for coming!"

"I wouldn't miss your wedding for the world," Weston assures her before turning his gaze to me. While I am sufficiently surprised by his presence, I can't help but notice he doesn't seem at all surprised to see me.

"Weston, surely you remember Princess Rosalind," Nicolás says.

I've been formally introduced to Lord Weston on more than one occasion, but we've not spent very much time in one another's company.

"Yes, of course I do. It's good to see you again, Your Highness." He steps forward to take my hand.

"And you, Lord Weston. I trust life is treating you well?"

"Very well, Your Highness. Thank you," he smiles. "And if I may say so, you are looking positively resplendent."

Oh, my. That's a bit much, isn't it?

"How kind of you," I say.

"Isn't she gorgeous? I was literally just telling her that before you guys walked in," Brittany claims.

I don't know if it's something in her tone or the way that she's watching Lord Weston and me like we're characters out of her favourite romantic comedy, but it's in this moment that everything becomes clear. I'm not here because Princess Isabel needs help with the wedding. I'm not even here to befriend Miss Walker.

I'm here to be courted.

CHAPTER THREE

"Did you know?" I demand, pacing back and forth across my bedroom while I interrogate my brother over the phone.

"How would I have known?" Robert asks.

"Because Mother and Father discuss everything with you."

"They discuss matters of state with me. Not your personal affairs," he corrects me. "And I don't know why you're getting so worked up. You were fully prepared and willing to marry the first man that Mum and Dad picked out for you."

"It's not the same."

"How?"

"Because I feel like they brought Lord Weston here as some sort of bizarre consolation prize. 'Oh, sorry you're not going to marry the future sovereign. But here, have a viscount.'"

"Now you're just being snobbish."

"I'm not trying to belittle him. I'm trying to say that it's *unfair* to him. He shouldn't allow himself to be subjected to such insult."

"Don't you think he would have refused to come had he really felt that way?"

"At the invitation of the royal family of San Cecilio? How could anyone refuse, regardless of the circumstances?"

"I don't know why you're resisting, but you are. If you were to calm down, take a deep breath, and think about it, you might come to realize that Lord Weston could be a very good match for you.

He's noble, respected, wealthy... Everything you could ask for in a husband."

"It just feels so... forced."

"And your betrothal to Nicolás didn't?" I don't have an answer for him. He takes my silence as permission to carry on. "You know, Rose, maybe this isn't really about Lord Weston. Maybe *you're* the one feeling second-rate."

"What is *that* supposed to mean?"

"Well, think about it. You were supposed to marry Nicolás, but he wanted someone else. You were supposed to become consort to the future monarch, and now that job is going to someone far less qualified. This young woman, nice as she may be, essentially waltzed right into what was supposed to be your life and replaced you."

I hadn't considered that. To tell you the truth, I'm not altogether familiar with feelings of inadequacy. I've always lived up to everyone's expectations, including my own. I obeyed every rule, completed every task, and have always taken great pride in my accomplishments and achievements.

Perhaps Robert is right. Perhaps Lord Weston isn't the one I pity.

Maybe, just maybe, it's me.

Dinner that night is a simple affair with Princess Isabel and Nicolás's father, Prince Vincent. We gather in the Great Hall in our semi-formal attire and sit down to a modest meal of grilled vegetables, pasta, and fish with raisins and pine nuts followed by chocolate pastries for dessert and a sweet

Moscatell to wash it all down. All the while, I'm trying to keep my mind open to new possibilities... and to cast aside every newfound doubt and insecurity that Robert so astutely identified earlier.

"You know, I've always wanted the opportunity to speak with you, to get to know you better," Lord Weston says to me over pastries and wine. "You just seem to be such a fascinating person."

"Why thank you. What a lovely compliment." Although, I'm not certain that it is altogether genuine. I'm afraid I lead a rather unremarkable existence. Since the very beginning, I've had my whole life planned out for me. That all seemed well and good until destiny saw fit to derail those plans.

"So. Tell me about yourself," Weston presses.

"Well... I enjoy music."

"Really? What sort?"

"All sorts. Classical, contemporary, popular. But I'm particularly keen on selections from Broadway."

"In that case, you must come visit me in London sometime. We can go to the West End. I'll take you to any show you'd like: *Phantom*, *The Lion King*, *Wicked*..."

"That sounds lovely." And a little extravagant.

"Well, then, it's a date," he smiles.

Oh, my. Is that what I've just agreed to? I suppose I should have figured it out sooner, but as it is, I've never been on a date. Not in the proper sense, anyway. Of course, Nicolás and I would attend the occasional ball or charity event together back when we were still betrothed, but it never felt the way it always seemed to in books or in movies.

After dinner, Prince Vincent and Princess Isabel bid all of us goodnight and adjourn to their bedchamber, leaving Nicolás, Weston, and me at the mercy of Brittany and her plans for what she promises will be a "festive and fun-filled evening."

"Okay, so I'm going to go change into my PJs and make the popcorn. Nick, you grab the blankets, Rosalind and Wes, why don't you pick out a Christmas movie? I've left a stack of my favourites in the green drawing room," Brittany instructs us. "Oh! And before I forget, does anyone want cocoa?"

"I do!" Nicolás grins.

"No, thank you," I reply.

"I think I'll pass, too," Weston says.

"Well, I'll make extra, just in case," Brittany assures us before bounding out of the room.

"She's wonderful, isn't she?" Nicolás sighs. "It is impossible not to love her."

"She is very sweet," I agree.

"So, you really *do* like her?" Nicolás asks, turning to face me.

"Oh... I... Well, I've only just met her. I still don't know her very well - "

"But you think she's sweet?"

"I do," I reply honestly.

"I'm so glad," Nicolás beams. "It's important to me that you like her. And it's important to her, too. She has so much respect for you. She really, really wants to be your friend."

Although I don't foresee the two of us becoming the kind of friends who call each other up at two in the morning or who share secrets over

20

cookie dough and rosé wine, I do acknowledge and accept that she is about to become a part of my life. Taking that into consideration, I would rather us be on good terms than not.

Instead of conveying all of this to Nicolás, however, I simply say, "I would like that, too."

"So, you'll stay tonight? For her movie night?"

After a long day of travel and excessive socializing, all I really want is to go to bed and sleep for fourteen hours. But Nicolás and Brittany have put forth so much effort into making their guests feel at home here in the castle. I would hate to come across as ill-mannered or ungrateful.

"Of course I will."

Again, Nicolás smiles and pulls me into a warm embrace.

"Thank you, Rosalind. Thank you."

Since neither Weston nor I is familiar with any of the Christmas movies that Brittany has set out for us, she selects a romantic holiday comedy. Although I have my doubts concerning the quality of this particular movie, I am willing to give it a chance for Nicolás's sake.

I've just taken my seat on the sofa when Brittany turns to me and asks, "Rosalind, what are you doing?"

"I'm... sitting down to watch the movie." I think that's the right answer.

"Not up there, you're not! Come on! We're camping out on the floor!" Brittany exclaims, dropping down onto a pile of blankets next to the fireplace.

"Wait. Really?"

"Yes! Come, join us! It's fun!" Nicolás insists, taking Brittany into his arms. All the while, Weston watches me with a keen smile and eager eyes.

"I don't know. I think I'd be more comfortable here on the sofa." I'm already wearing my dressing gown in front of two very recent acquaintances. I can only imagine how vulnerable I would feel sitting with them on the floor.

"Then I'll come sit on the sofa next to you," Weston announces, rising up from his makeshift throne of pillows.

"Oh, that's really not necessary," I tell him.

"Nonsense. I insist. I hate to see a Princess lonely."

Oh, dear God.

As if that doesn't make me feel uneasy enough, Brittany turns around to watch as he joins me on the sofa. Then she catches my eye and winks.

It's going to be a very long night, isn't it?

CHAPTER FOUR

Her Royal Heartbreak: Princess Rosalind Is In San Cecilio!

Can Rosalind Win Nicolás Back? 10 Reason Why We Think She Can!

Rosalind's Revenge: Brittany's Bitter Rival Hopes to Stop the Royal Wedding!

It's a long way from Once Upon a Time to Happily Ever After, especially when the Princess who was supposed to marry your Prince comes knocking on your castle door.

Her Royal Highness, Rosalind of Mondovia arrived in Valoña, the capital city of San Cecilio, two days ago and has been staying at the castle with Prince Nicolás and his bride-to-be, Miss Brittany Walker. While a spokesperson for the royal family insists that the Princess is there at Nicolás and Brittany's invitation, insider sources claim that she is, in fact, on a personal mission to take back what she believes is her rightful place by the Prince's side.

"She's definitely hoping to win him back," says an unnamed source. "She's a beautiful and strong-minded person who is used to getting her way. And she's not going to let Nicolás... or the Crown... go without a fight."

Sounds like this Princess means business! But what do we really know about her?

Born Rosalind Elisabetta Marie Claremont, she is the second child and only daughter of Their Majesties, King David and Queen Mathilde of Mondovia. Her brother, Robert Arthur Gabriel Claremont, is next in line to inherit the throne.

Rosalind grew up a smart and successful child, very focused on her studies and extracurricular activities, *such as equestrianism and music lessons. It is said that the Princess is a fine singer and a skilled pianist.*

Unfortunately for the young Royal, no amount of talent or intelligence will earn her a Kingdom to call her own. Is it really any wonder she finds herself vying for Nicolás's hand, if not his heart?

It's my third morning in San Cecilio and I am rapidly approaching my wit's end.

First, Princess Isabel, who has been overseeing Brittany's Princess Lessons (yes, there are such things), asked if I might like to sit in to offer encouragement and additional guidance. I agreed, thinking it would be a simple, perhaps even enjoyable undertaking. What I didn't anticipate, however, was how resistant Brittany is to traditional etiquette. She questions the merit of nearly every rule, every regulation, every piece of practical protocol. Not because she intends to be rude, but because it is all so very foreign and nonsensical to her.

Then, there's Lord Weston. While I appreciate his interest and am flattered by his persistence, having him constantly hovering is, in a word, overwhelming. It's as though he's already decided that we're going to be together; inviting me to London, making plans for the new year. He's even gone so far as to refer to me as "his" Princess. It was only then that I was finally forced to say something.

"Forgive me, Lord Weston, but I am not *your* Princess."

He began backpedaling immediately.

"Oh, no. Of course, you belong to no one, Your Highness. I merely intended it as a phrase of endearment. You know, my Darling... My Dear... My Princess."

"Well, be that as it may, it's not a phrase that I fancy."

"Yes, yes, of course. I understand. I do apologize. I hope you know I meant no disrespect."

"I do. Thank you."

If that's not enough, Brittany parents are scheduled to land in San Cecilio this afternoon, so the entire staff is hustling and bustling about the castle making sure everything is in order, not just for their arrival, but for the banquet that Prince Vincent and Prince Isabel are hosting tonight to welcome them into the family.

Now, on top of all of that, the international press has finally caught wind of my stay here in San Cecilio. And of course, they're having a field day at my expense.

I can't do this anymore. I need to get out of here. Take a day off.

But how?

Perhaps I can feign an illness. I'd be confined to my bedroom, but it would at least give me the afternoon all to myself. Or maybe I could climb out of my window and escape into the courtyard. Only then, I run the risk of breaking my leg or getting caught by the royal guards or possibly both. Maybe I should just ask Sophie if any of the staff members here know of any secret passageways out of the castle. Granted, that may be a bit of a stretch, but I'm feeling rather desperate.

If only escaping from a royal residence were as simple as walking out the front door.

"Good morning, Your Highness," Sophie greets me, gliding into the room.

"Sophie, if you were going to sneak out of a castle, how would you do it?"

"Is this going to be one of those conversations that I'm supposed to pretend didn't happen?"

"If you don't mind."

"All right. Well, if I needed to get away, I suppose I'd make up some sort of plausible excuse. You know, like I need to run to the shops. Then again, it's a bit easier for someone like me to leave without causing too much of a stir."

She's right, of course. For the most part, members of the staff are able to come and go as they please. It's the royal visitors they like to keep under lock and key.

Heaving a defeated sigh, I turn to gaze out my window just in time to see a small bus pulling up to the front gate. It's only then that I remember that the castle is open to guided tours on select days of the week, and it looks like today is one of them.

"Urgh. More people," I groan.

"At least you don't have to meet with them."

"But I'll still know they're here."

"You know, you'd think that with the wedding preparations and the Walkers arriving later on this afternoon, the tours would be canceled," Sophie comments.

"Exactly. As if the energy here isn't chaotic enough."

Wait a minute...

"Right. Now, if anyone should ask, I'm not feeling well but it's nothing a little bed rest won't cure."

"Are you sure about this?" Sophie asks, helping me change into jeans and an oversized winter coat.

"For the most part."

"What if you get caught?"

"So I get caught. What are they going to do? Lock me in the stocks?"

"What if you're recognized? Or kidnapped? Maybe I should go with you...."

"No! I need you here to cover for me," I remind her. "I'm not going to go far. Just far enough. And I'll have my phone with me."

I check my reflection in the mirror one last time before heading out. Along with the coat, I've donned a knitted souvenir hat bearing the flag of San Cecilio and a pair of glasses that Sophie sometimes uses for reading. If someone were to look hard enough, they might recognize me, but as long as I keep a low profile, I should be able to hide in plain sight.

Now, all that's left is to wait for the opportune moment to sneak into the tour group and waltz out the front door like I'm just another vacationer, here for the sights and photo ops.

The group itself is relatively small, no more than twelve people or so. Still, I think there are enough visitors here to help me blend in.

They've just passed through the library when I decide to take my shot. No one is looking. If I can just tag along behind the last two tourists, slip in as though I'd been there all along, I might just be able to pull this off -

Thud!

In my haste, I fail to watch my step and my foot accidentally catches a small end table near the door, creating a domino effect that topples three books, a small picture frame, and, to my utter horror, an antique candelabra that tumbles over the edge and falls to the ground with a loud *clang*!

"What was that?" the man leading the tour bellows. He's a man of large stature with a balding head and a mustache. He looks more like a cartoon wrestler than a castle tour guide.

"This poor girl tripped over a table," one of the visitors, an older woman, informs him. "Are you all right, dear?"

"Yes, yes, I'm fine. Thank you."

"Young lady, what were you thinking?" the tour guide demands.

"I... er..." I clear my throat. "I wasn't looking and I... I'm terribly sorry."

"Well, don't let it happen again," he scolds me.

"Yes, sir."

He glowers at me for a moment longer before finally, he turns around and carries on with the tour. I heave a shuddering sigh of relief.

"Don't worry, dear," the older woman tells me. "The first time I toured a castle, I ended up shattering a crystal goblet they had on display in the kitchen."

"Really?" I ask, feeling a little better about my thoughtless blunder.

"Oh, yes. This sort of thing happens far more often than these stuffy tour guides would ever want you to know," she says, smiling up at me. Then, she takes a second glance. "Have you been with us this whole time?"

So much for keeping a low profile.

CHAPTER FIVE

I can't believe it. I did it. And oh, I am so glad that I did.

The streets of downtown Valoña are sparkling with Christmas lights and holiday spirit and for the first time in quite a while, I feel like I can finally breathe. And as it just so happens, the air smells like cinnamon and evergreen. Delightful.

Although I've visited Valoña many times before, this is my first Christmas here and everything about it is pure magic, from the choir singing carols on the steps of the courthouse to the Christmas trees blinking on every corner. The shops themselves are equally festive with their holiday displays and decorations.

As I stop to admire a three-story, frosted gingerbread house inside a bakery window, I realize I'm only just around the block from my favourite local bookstore; the perfect place to lie low for a few hours.

Glancing around just to make sure I'm not being watched or followed, I make the short trek to the bookstore, where employees are just putting the finishing touches on a Christmas tree constructed entirely out of green and red paperbacks.

"How clever," I declare, far more loudly than I intended.

The girl trimming the book tree turns to look at me.

"Why thank you, Miss. Is there anything I can help you find today?"

"Oh, no. No thank you. I'm just looking."

"Well, if you need assistance, my name is Gloria," she says with a bright smile.

"Thank you, Gloria."

Casually, I meander back to the aisles marked *Ficción/Fiction*. I really don't need to buy any new books. My personal library back home is literally overflowing with books that I have yet to read, but sometimes, when I find myself surrounded by new titles and the smell of fresh, unread pages, I can't help myself.

I select a few books that friends have recommended to me and a few others that catch my eye from the shelves before carefully making my way to the small reading nook near the back of the store.

Unfortunately, carefully isn't careful enough.

"Oof!"

For the second time, I'm startled and caught completely off guard when I collide with something standing in my path. This time, a living, breathing human being. At least this morning it was just a table.

"Oh! Oh no! I am so sorry," I gasp. "I do hope that you'll... you'll forgive..." But for what may very well be the first time in my life, I'm rendered speechless.

The person staring down at me, the one I've nearly just trampled to the ground, is the handsomest young man I have ever seen. I've spent my life surrounded by Princes and Lords, many of whom I've never given a second glance. Yet this young man manages to take my breath away with a single look.

He's tall, much taller than Nicolás, with dark blond hair that's tousled like he's also been wearing a hat, and about a week's growth of unshaven scruff on his sharp, angular jawline. However, it's in his eyes, those beautiful eyes as blue as the winter sky, that I truly lose myself.

"No, no, you're fine. Don't worry about it," he assures me. "Are *you* okay? Do you need some help?"

"Help?" I ask, still in a daze. That's when I realize that I'm no longer holding my stack of books. Now, they're strewn around in a scattered mess on the floor. "Oh, right. My books. Er... no. It's all right. I can get them."

"Please, allow me," he insists, bending down on one knee to help collect them and pausing to read each title as he goes. "Ah. Good choice," he says, holding up the book so I can see. It's *The Giver* by Lois Lowry.

"I've been meaning to read it for ages," I admit.

"You mean you didn't read it when you were in school?" he asks. It's only then that I pick up on his accent. He's American.

"No. Our curriculum was... rather rigorous."

"Well, I think you're really going to enjoy it. I read it for English class when I was fourteen and it's still one of my favourites."

"I'm glad to know that," I smile.

After he's gathered up all of the books, he rises back up to his full height.

"Do you need a hand carrying all of these?" he asks. I'm pleasantly taken aback.

"I appreciate it, but I don't want to inconvenience you."

"Not an inconvenience at all. Besides, I would hate for you to run into another innocent bystander."

"Oh, how gallant of you," I blush.

"That's actually my nickname back home. Mr. Gallant."

"Really?"

"No," he laughs and I realize with a start that he's flirting with me.

I'm not used to this. Most men are polite to me because they're required to be. But this young man has no idea who I am. He sees only a girl in a bookstore. A girl with questionable fashion sense, at that. And yet, he still seems to like me.

"So, what brings you to San Cecilio?" I ask him.

"Oh, you know. Heard it's the place to be this time of year."

"Is this your first visit?"

"I've been once before. Last summer," he answers. "And what about you? I can tell by your accent you're not a local."

"I... have family who lives here." It's almost the truth. And who knows? So many royal lines are interwoven, I may very well be distantly related to Nicolás and Isabel.

"Visiting for the holidays?"

"Yes."

"That's cool. So, where are you from?"

"Er... Italy." Okay, so that's a little less true. But my mother is of Italian and French descent. And Mondovia is just a hop, skip, and a jump across the Adriatic Sea. "And you?"

"Right now, I'm living in Columbus, Ohio."

"Oh, how lovely."

"I guess it can be," he says as he goes to set my books down. We've finally reached the reading nook, a cozy space made up of two sofas and a coffee table. For the winter, the store has even provided fleece blankets. "So, what's your name?"

"I'm Ro - " I catch myself just in time. Rosalind isn't exactly a name you hear every day. "Rose. My name is Rose."

"Beautiful," my handsome Knight in shining armor smiles, holding out his hand. "I'm Zach."

"Is that short for Zachary?"

"Yeah, but please, just call me Zach," he says.

"Very well... Zach."

"You don't like it, do you?"

"Not particularly." I tease. "It's just not very refined."

"Well, between you and me, I'm not either," he winks.

Oh God, I'm in trouble.

"So, Rose," he continues. "If I were looking for the best meal in Valoña, where would you, as someone relatively familiar with the area, suggest I find it?"

That's a good question. My honest answer would be the castle, but since that's not exactly an option, I'll go with the second-best option.

"About two blocks over, there's a small cafe called Donna's. They serve breakfast all day, and the atmosphere inside is very homey. It's not the fanciest dining experience, but it's my favourite."

"Sounds perfect," Zach says. "Are you hungry?"

I am, but I'm not sure I should admit that. I have absolutely no business running around a busy city with a man I've just met. No matter how beautiful his eyes are.

That's it, then. I've made my decision. I will politely decline.

"Actually, yes."

No! No, that's the wrong answer!

"Would you like to join me?"

No, I would not like to join you. I don't know you at all and I have no reason to trust you. Now if you'll excuse me, I must be getting back to the castle.

"I'd be delighted."

The atmosphere inside Donna's is warm and comfortable, with fresh bread baking in the ovens, small vases of flowers on every table, and a fire dancing in the hearth. The building itself is dimly lit, which is both fortuitous and inadvertently romantic. Not that this is a date. It absolutely is not.

"So how long are you here in Valoña?" I ask Zachary - er, Zach - while we wait for our server to return with our drink orders.

"Just a few days. I'll have to be getting back to work."

"What do you do?"

"I'm a vet."

"A vet? Like a war veteran?"

"A veterinarian," he grins, his eyes sparkling with golden firelight.

"Oh, how wonderful. So, you take care of dogs and cats?"

"I actually work for the Columbus Zoo."

Okay, *that* is very impressive.

"How many animals is that?"

"About seven thousand," he answers.

"And you treat... all of them?"

"Well, not just me. We have a fantastic team of other veterinarians and technicians. And of course, the keepers."

"Do you have a favourite animal?"

"Well, I don't think I'm supposed to but..." He reaches into his pocket and pulls out his cell phone. He then proceeds to show me photo after photo of elephants, polar bears, orangutans, gorillas, and red pandas.

"These pictures are incredible. Did you take them all yourself?" I ask.

"Oh, no. I stole most of them off the website. My pictures always somehow turn out blurry."

"That's a shame."

"Well, there's only so much you can expect from a camera phone," he grins. "One day, though, I'm going to buy myself a really nice camera and I'm going to take it on safari in Africa."

"Africa is amazing. Have you ever been?"

"No. But it's number one on my bucket list."

"Your what?"

"You've never heard of a bucket list?"

"Is it a list of things to do that you draw out of a bucket?"

"No," he laughs. "It's a list of goals that you have for your life. You know, before you kick the bucket."

"I don't think I've ever heard that expression."

"Maybe it's an American thing," he says. "Speaking of which, we have spent far too much time talking about me. Tell me about you."

Oh, not this again. Can't we talk about something that I'm trying very hard *not* to lie about?

"What would you like to know?"

"Well, you know what I do. What do you do?"

Wow, I walked right into that one, didn't I?

"I'm... sort of between jobs right now."

"Okay..." He's expecting me to elaborate. Fantastic.

"My dad is... very involved with the government, you see, and he's been trying to help me out. We just haven't really found the right fit yet."

"Is that what you'd like to do? Work for the government?"

"It's really all I've ever known," I answer honestly. "Then again, there might not be a place for me."

"And if there isn't?"

"I don't know."

"Well, the good news is you've got plenty of time to figure it out," he says. Then he smiles and looks at me with eyes so captivating and sincere that for just a moment, I forget that whatever "it" is, it isn't up to me.

By the time Zach and I finish eating, it's nearly one o'clock in the afternoon. I've been away from the castle for almost three hours. Any longer, and I know I'll be pushing my luck. Besides, the Walkers are due to arrive soon and I've just remembered that I'm expected at a cocktail reception scheduled for them an hour before the banquet. That only gives me just enough time to get back to the castle, shower, dress, and tend to my appearance before making my way down to the gold drawing room where the family entertains.

I'm already dreading it. I'm dreading the small talk and the curious glances and the unspoken questions concerning my presence.

But most of all, I'm dreading saying goodbye to Zach.

We've just stepped out of Donna's and are lingering on the sidewalk in front of the building. The streets of the city are as crowded and lively as before, yet somehow, it feels as though we're the only two people in the world.

"Zach, thank you for your company this afternoon. I've truly enjoyed it," I tell him in earnest.

"So have I," he grins. "Maybe I'll run into you again. Or, you know, maybe *you'll* run into me."

"Funny," I remark, casting him a sidelong glance.

"I thought it was."

"Just so you know, I'm usually not that clumsy."

"Whatever you say, Rose."

He's gazing down at me now in a way that no man has ever looked at me before. Like there are no rules to abide by, no titles to respect, no protocol to be broken. In his eyes, I'm just an ordinary girl.

And I think, if I were to ask him, he would kiss me.

Not that I would ever consider such a thing. It wouldn't be at all appropriate.

"Well listen, I really do need to be going," I tell him. "Before I do though..."

"Yeah?"

"And I'd like to preface this by saying that I've never done anything like this before, but since I probably won't ever see you again..." My heart is fluttering so quickly I can barely catch my breath. "May I kiss you?"

Now it's his turn to blush. Sheepishly, he smiles down at his shoes before lifting his gaze back up to me. Then, at long last, he nods.

Trembling, I take a small step toward him. I can feel his warmth radiating from the coat that he wears as I reach up with deft fingers to stroke his beard. Then, certain that I have no idea what I'm doing, I rise up on my tiptoes and press my lips gently to his. It's a kiss as soft and serene as the snowflakes that surround us, and although it's over within seconds, it's a moment I know will stay with me forever.

Zach, on the other hand, looks pensive and - dare I say it - mildly unimpressed.

"*That* wasn't a real kiss," he says.

And with that, he sweeps me up into his arms and lowers his mouth to mine. This time, the kiss lingers, and before I can stop myself, I'm wrapping my arms around his shoulders and kissing him back with the kind of passion I've only ever witnessed in movies.

He kisses me once, twice, three times more before he lets me go, and I drift back down to Earth feeling dizzy, dreamy, and weightless. Finally, I open my eyes and take one last look at his handsome face, endeavoring to memorize his every feature.

There isn't enough time in the world. And I'm already late.

"Goodbye, Zach," I whisper.

He smiles.

"Merry Christmas, Rose."

CHAPTER SIX

Preparations for the Walkers' arrival are in full swing by the time I stroll casually back into the castle as though I'd been gone no longer than a mere moment or two. Garland adorns every hall, wreaths decorate the windows, and I've counted no less than seven twinkling Christmas trees on my way back to my bedroom.

I've no sooner slipped inside than Sophie appears, breathing a sigh of relief.

"Oh, Your Highness, thank Heavens it's you," she says. "Lord Weston has been coming around every twenty minutes to ask how you're doing. I think he truly believes you've contracted the plague."

"Goodness, we can't have that," I remark lightly.

"If you don't mind me saying, he seems to be very taken with you."

"Yes, well... he is a lovely person."

Something in my tone must give me away, because Sophie raises a curious eyebrow and looks at me.

"Are you all right?" she asks.

"Yes. Why?"

"I don't know. There's something... different about you."

I shrug.

"Must be the fresh Iberian air."

I could tell her the truth about my venture into Valoña and my rendezvous with Zach, and a part of me is very tempted to do so. But there's another part that wants to keep him, and every moment with him, all to myself.

Sophie is still watching me with suspicion, but before she can question me further, someone knocks on the door.

"Come in," I call.

The door opens and Lord Weston peaks inside.

"Ah, there you are," he smiles. "I was beginning to worry about you. How are you feeling?"

"Much better. Thank you," I answer.

"I'm glad to hear it. You look... comfortable."

It isn't until he says so that I remember I'm still dressed in my tourist disguise.

"Ah, yes. I was just about to change."

"I'm sorry, that came out wrong. Please know that I didn't mean to offend. I'm just... not accustomed to seeing the Princess of Mondovia in blue jeans," he explains. "You look beautiful, as always."

"That's very sweet." He actually looks rather handsome himself in his tuxedo. Not nearly as handsome, though, as Zach had looked in his casual, everyday attire. "Is there anything I can do for you?"

"Yes, actually," he says. "I was wondering if I might escort you to the banquet tonight? It is a formal affair, after all, and I would be honoured if you would let me accompany you."

It may be a formal affair, but it is also a family affair, which makes it far more personal and intimate than a state dinner or a charity reception. However, I suppose it would be nice to have someone there with me, if for no other reason than to prove to the

Walkers that I am not, in fact, there to try and snake Nicolás away from their daughter.

"That would be wonderful. Thank you, Lord Weston."

"It's my pleasure, Your Highness. Truly," he insists. "Well then, I suppose I should let you get ready."

"Indeed."

"I'll see you in a little while."

"Yes, you shall," I promise.

His face lights up. Then he bows politely and retreats back out into the hallway. Watching him leave, an image of Zach smiling amidst the swirling snowflakes flashes before my eyes. Flustered, I turn away and look to Sophie for a sense of stability.

"Are you sure you're feeling all right?" she asks.

This time, I have no answer for her.

By the time I step out of the shower, I've managed to regain most of my composure. The hot water seems to have cleared my head and although my memories of Zach are still quite vivid, he's no longer at the forefront of my mind. My afternoon with him was a chapter straight out of a fairy tale, but now the spell is broken and my winter boots and blue jeans have transformed back into sparkling slippers and a crimson evening gown.

"I think that should just about do it," Sophie murmurs to herself as she styles my long brown locks up into an elegant bun. "There's just one more thing..." She disappears into my closet only to return moments later bearing a black velvet box.

"What is that?"

"An early Christmas present from your brother," Sophie answers, opening the box to reveal a dazzling diamond tiara. I've worn tiaras before, of course, but they've always been on loan to me from my mother or from the Royal Estate.

"Oh, it's beautiful," I sigh, thoroughly moved by Robert's thoughtful gesture.

"He hoped you would like it," Sophie says as she deftly lifts the tiara out of its box and fastens it into my hair.

"It's perfect." And it is. Trimmed in silver, it's neither too large nor too ostentatious. It's simple and stylish, but it sparkles just enough to catch the eye.

After she's certain that the tiara is secure, Sophie steps around to face me.

"Don't let them forget who you are," she tells me. "And don't you forget, either."

They're words I didn't realize I needed to hear until after they're spoken. I'm not oblivious to the fact that I may be met tonight with scorn and skepticism. I know there are those who will continue to doubt my intentions. But I made a promise to be there for Nicolás, for Isabel, and for Miss Walker. And a Princess always keeps her promises.

At precisely ten minutes to five, I emerge from my bedroom and go to meet Lord Weston at the foot of the grand staircase. He's already there, waiting.

"Wow, Rosalind," he breathes. "You look stunning."

"Thank you." Since tonight is a night of celebration and welcome, I'm willing to overlook his informal greeting. Once. "Well, shall we?"

"Let's," he grins, offering me his arm. As I take it, however, I can't help but notice his eyes drifting upward from my face to the glittering tiara above it. His gaze lingers for only a moment before he catches himself. Then, without another word, he turns his attention forward and leads me into the gold drawing room, a bright, enchanting space at the heart of the castle.

There are more guests present than I'd anticipated. Nicolás and Brittany are here, of course, as are Princess Isabel and Prince Vincent. They're standing at the center of the room, chatting with a fine-looking older couple I presume to be Mr. and Mrs. Walker. I also recognize a few of Nicolás's aunts, uncles, and cousins.

"Princess Rosalind, what a pleasure to see you," Nicolás's Aunt Vanessa says to me.

"And you, Your Grace," I reply. "How have you been?"

"Oh, just wonderful, my dear. Thank you for asking. How are you?"

"I'm splendid. Very much enjoying my time here in San Cecilio."

"So I can see," Vanessa smirks, eyeing Lord Weston with delight and curiosity. "And who might this be?"

"Oh, I'm sorry. Please forgive me. Your Grace, this is Lord Weston Bentley. Lord Weston, Duchess Vanessa DeCagney, Nicolás's Aunt."

"It's an honour," Weston grins and takes Vanessa's hand.

"Likewise," Vanessa smiles before looking back to me. "It's so wonderful to see you so happy. I'll admit that I've been rather worried about you."

"Thank you. I appreciate your thoughts. But I assure you I am doing very well."

"I am so glad to hear it," Vanessa says. "I hope you know that no matter what, you will always be family to us."

"And you to me," I tell her.

"Rosalind!" I turn just in time to see Brittany approaching me, her arms outstretched. She looks positively breathtaking in a shimmering silver evening gown and diamond headpiece. "I'm so happy you're here! I heard you weren't feeling very well this morning."

"I just needed to rest."

"Oh, I totally get it. I have been completely exhausted for like, the past two weeks. And with Christmas and the wedding only two weeks away, life is only going to get even more hectic. In the best possible way, of course," she smiles. "And Weston, you are looking *very* handsome tonight. Doesn't he look handsome, Rosalind?"

"Indeed," I answer.

"Thank you, ladies," Lord Weston blushes. "Brittany, has your family arrived?"

"They have! And I'm dying for them to meet you. Come on, let me introduce you!"

She guides us across the room to where Nicolás stands, chatting with the same distinguished couple as before. Mr. Walker is tall and heavyset, with a headful of white hair and thick-rimmed glasses. Mrs. Walker, on the other hand, is short and delicate like her daughter, with auburn hair that has clearly been artificially coloured and perfectly polished fingernails.

"Mom, Dad!" she calls, flouncing up to them. "I'd like you to meet Lord Weston Bentley and Her Royal Highness, Princess Rosalind of Mondovia."

"It's lovely to - "

But the words die on my lips as another young man steps forward to join our gathering. He's tall, fit, and devastatingly handsome. And the moment he recognizes me, his eyes widen and his brows furrow in what I can only describe as pure shock.

"Oh, Zach! There you are!" Brittany grins, blessedly oblivious to the stunned look on both of our faces. "Weston, Rosalind, this is my big brother, Zachary Walker. Zach, these are our good friends, Lord Weston and Princess Rosalind."

"How do you do?" Weston greets him.

"Uh... fine, thanks," Zach answers half-heartedly, his eyes still locked on my face.

I suppose I should say something, too, so I clear my throat and extend my hand.

"It's very nice to meet you, Zachary."

"No, no. The pleasure is mine... *Your Highness*," he replies, taking my hand and bowing ever so slightly.

"It's funny... Miss Walker never mentioned that she... she had a brother." My voice is trembling. This is not good.

"Oh, I'm guessing there are a lot of things you don't know about each other."

Oh, my God.

Did he *really* just say that to me?

"Zach, don't be snarky," Brittany scolds. "You'll have to forgive him. He's not really into all of this."

"But he is *very* grateful and honoured to be here. As we all are," Mrs. Walker assures us, enunciating every syllable.

"And we are honoured to have you here," Nicolás grins. "You are family, now, after all."

Family.

Oh, my *God*.

They really are family now. Zach's sister is marrying Nicolás. The strange man I snogged in the streets this morning is about to become my ex-fiancé's *brother-in-law*. How is this happening? Dear God, tell me this isn't happening.

"Rosalind, are you feeling all right?" Weston asks.

"Yes, of course," I answer far too quickly.

"You do look a little pale," Brittany observes. "Do you need some water?"

"No, no, I'm fine. Really."

"Well, maybe you should at least sit down," Brittany suggests.

"The Princess was feeling a touch under the weather this morning," Weston explains to the Walkers.

"Oh, dear. Then maybe you should find a place to sit down," Mrs. Walker says to me.

Zach, on the other hand, raises a rather judgmental eyebrow in my direction and realization hits me once again. Only this time, it hits like a sledgehammer.

He's angry with me.

Well, perhaps not *angry*, but he certainly isn't pleased. Of course, I can only imagine why. I lied to him about practically everything; who I am, why I'm here, where I'm from, and what I do. I couldn't even be bothered to give him my real name. Now, on top of all of that, he finds out I've been lying to everyone around me as well.

This is not at all the beginning of a fairy tale romance.

Not that it was ever the beginning of anything. I have absolutely no future with Zach. I never did.

And now I know I never will.

CHAPTER SEVEN

At a quarter to six, guests begin migrating into the great hall for the banquet. Eager to put as much distance between Zach and myself as possible, I follow the crowd and sit myself near the far end of the table. I'm certain that, as the guests of honour, the Walkers will be seated next to Princess Isabel and Prince Vincent at the head, so I should be safe from any scathing glances or unspoken questions.

"Rosalind. What are you doing?"

Or perhaps not.

I glance up to see Nicolás standing over me, looking rather amused.

"I'm sitting."

"Not here. Come, you and Weston will sit with Brittany and me."

"Oh, that's very kind of you, but I... I think I would be more comfortable if I were to just stay here."

"Is this about Zach?"

"Of course not. Why would you ask such a thing?"

"Because you seemed... nervous when you were around him. Has he done something to offend you?"

"No. No, not at all. I just... don't think I should be around him."

"Why not?"

"... Because Mother warned me that American men are scoundrels."

And that is when Nicolás throws his head back and laughs.

"Perhaps some of them are, but Zach is a good man. Did you know that he takes care of animals?" he asks. "Come on. Give him a chance."

"Very well," I sigh.

"That's the spirit," Nicolás smiles, offering me his hand. I take it and allow him to escort me to the head of the table where Brittany and Weston are already seated across from the Walker family.

Everyone rises, of course, when Princess Isabel and Prince Vincent make their entrance. As daughter of the late sovereign and reigning monarch of San Cecilio, Princess Isabel takes her place at the head of the table, with her consort, Prince Vincent, directly to her right and her heir, Nicolás, to her left.

"Before we begin, a word of welcome," Princess Isabel proclaims. "To you, our beloved family and cherished friends, thank you for your presence here tonight, and for sharing in our joy as we celebrate not only this Christmas season, but also the marriage of our son, Prince Nicolás to Miss Brittany Walker." Princess Isabel pauses to exchange a fond look with her son and future daughter-in-law. "And to the Walker family, it is our honour and privilege to welcome you here tonight, for you have provided us with one of our greatest blessings: a beautiful, kind, and compassionate young woman who loves our Nicolás with all her heart. As a mother, that is all I can ever hope to ask for my son. So, thank you. And welcome to the family." Princess Isabel then raises her crystal goblet of wine in a toast. "Now, I invite you all to be seated and to enjoy your evening!"

Somehow, in spite of everything that has transpired this evening, I manage to find myself smiling. That's one of the many things I love about Princess Isabel. When you're a guest at her table, it is impossible not to smile.

Throughout the course of the banquet, conversations are kept light and although I am seated directly across from Zach, neither of us exchanges so much as a glance all evening. Granted, I do steal a glimpse here and there, but every time, he's either engaged in conversation or staring down at his plate. It seems he's as keen to avoid me as I am him.

After dinner, Princess Isabel invites a select few to stay for wine and dessert. Although I truly am beginning to feel out of sorts after a long and trying day, I also know that it would be rude to decline. So, taking Lord Weston's arm once more, I follow him, Nicolás, and Brittany into the parlour, a cozy, dimly-lit room that immediately puts me in mind of the atmosphere at Donna's... and my afternoon with Zach.

He's there, of course, along with his parents and one of Nicolás's female cousins who seems to be attempting to strike up a conversation with him. He answers her questions politely, but I can tell, even from across the room, that he's distracted.

While my friends disperse throughout the parlour, I slip away and settle into a chair by the fireplace. If I can just sit here long enough to be seen, and to thank Princess Isabel for a delightful evening, then perhaps I'll be able to take my leave.

"Your Highness?" I glance up to see a young man holding a silver platter of wine glasses.

"Oh, no thank you," I smile at him.

"Sir?" he addresses someone behind me.

"No thanks," a very familiar voice answers.

I turn just in time to see Zach taking a seat in the chair next to me.

"So, I guess this explains a few things," he comments.

"Such as?"

"Your perfect posture, for one. Your indirect answers about your upbringing and being 'between jobs...'" he lists. "Why you assumed you would never see me again..."

"I guess that sort of backfired, didn't it?" I offer a weary smile, hoping to lighten the mood.

"To be fair, I thought the same thing," he admits.

"Is that why you told me you were only in town for a few days?"

"Easier than telling you I flew in for my sister's royal wedding," he reasons. "So why are *you* really here?"

"What do you mean?"

"Well, if all those news articles are to be believed, you're scheming to stop the wedding and win Nicolás back."

Oh, so that's why he was acting so antagonistic toward me earlier. Because he's read those wretched reports.

"Do *you* think that's why I'm here?"

"The girl I met this afternoon didn't strike me as the scheming type."

"Good. Because I'm not," I assure him. "I came at Princess Isabel's invitation. And my mother's request."

"So when you said that you were visiting family..."

"It was almost true. My mother and Princess Isabel have been friends for years. Our families are very close."

"Still? Even after everything that's happened with Nicolás and my sister?"

I nod.

"I know the tabloids and magazines were trying to sell the story that the monarchs were feuding, hearts were broken, and that ending an arranged engagement would cause some grand political upheaval between nations. But our betrothal was always more of a personal decision between our parents than any sort of political agreement."

"So, there were no cries for vengeance or duels to the death atop a jagged cliff?" he grins.

"Of course not. This isn't *Game of Thrones*."

"Actually, I was thinking more of *The Princess Bride*."

"That's another book I've been told to read."

"Well, if I'm being completely honest, I haven't read that one either. But the movie's great."

"Maybe we can request it if your sister hosts another one of her movies nights."

Zach chuckles under his breath.

"Typical Britt. She moves into a castle and all she wants to do is watch movies and build blanket forts."

I'm about to assure him that it's all part of her charm when I notice someone approaching out of the corner of my eye. I glance around to see Lord Weston approaching with two glasses of wine.

"Thought you might like a drink," he announces, offering one to me. Then, as though he's only just noticed that I'm not alone, he says, "Ah. Hello again, Mr. Walker."

"It's Doctor, actually," Zach corrects him.

"Oh, right. Your animals. I remember reading about them."

"You do?" I ask. "When?"

"After Nicolás and Brittany first announced their engagement. Every media outlet in the world had something new to say about the Princess-to-be and her family. Actually, there were a couple of articles written exclusively about you, weren't there?"

"Can't believe everything you read online," Zach tells him. "I was reminded of that about five minutes ago."

"I see. So, it's not true then that you broke up with your long-term girlfriend to pursue - how do I phrase this? - nobler prospects?"

If he's hoping to intimidate Zach, it isn't working. Zach remains as calm and confident as ever. Even, dare I say, a little amused.

"You know, I think it's just about time for bed," he says, rising up out of his chair. I can't help but notice that, at his full height, he towers almost a head above Weston. I'm certain Weston is well aware of it, too.

"Ah, quite right. You've had a long day, after all. Probably jet-lagged," Weston comments, stepping aside to allow Zach to pass. "Have a good night."

"Yeah, you too," Zach replies before turning his attention back to me. "Goodnight, Your Highness."

I smile back at him.

"Sleep well, Dr. Walker."

It isn't long after Zach goes to bed that I also turn in for the night. Of course, I'm not at all surprised when Weston offers to walk me to my room. And I hope I'm not wrong to let him. I know that he's still the smart match. But I also know that his isn't the face I'll be seeing in my dreams tonight.

"So, what did you and Mr. Walker discuss this evening?" he asks as we ascend the grand staircase.

"Oh, you know. This and that."

"He wasn't disrespectful, was he?"

The question is so absurd I don't know whether to laugh or take offense.

"Certainly not. He was the perfect gentleman."

"Good," Weston says, though his tone is short. "You know, I've met his type. In London."

"And what type might that be?"

"Cocky. Confident. The Hollywood type."

"Actually, he lives in Ohio." Not that I'm all that familiar with American geography. I do know that Hollywood is in California, though.

"They come from all over, but they're all the same. They think they deserve the world and all because of their handsome features. And if you don't believe me, look him up online," he advises as we come to a stop outside of my bedroom door.

I'm halfway into my room before I turn back around to face him.

"You may recall, Lord Weston, that the press has not always been kind to me, either," I point out. "Goodnight."

And with that, I close the door and leave him to dwell while I prepare myself for bed.

Once I've changed into my blue satin nightgown and brushed my teeth, I settle in beneath the heavy blankets and embroidered comforter. Then, I pick my phone up from the nightstand, connect to the internet, and type Zach's name into the search engine.

The articles that Weston referenced appear almost immediately.

Princess-To-Be Brittany Walker Has a Brother... AND HE'S HOT!

Prince Charming Who? Turns Out Zachary Walker is the Fairest of Them All!

Ten Delectable Details About Brittany's Dreamy Brother!

We've all heard the story of how American travel agent Brittany Walker took the trip of a lifetime to San Cecilio and won the heart of a real-life Prince. But what do we know about her older brother, Zachary, who looks like he walked straight out of a fairy tale himself?

1. He's a doctor. More specifically, he's a veterinarian... FOR EXOTIC WILDLIFE. You read that right. Zach has worked at three different zoos around the country, caring for thousands of animals, including endangered species such as African elephants, gorillas, giraffes, California sea lions, and even polar bears!

2. He's an avid reader. A few of his favorite titles include The Giver *by Lois Lowry,* The Lord of the

Rings *Trilogy by J. R. R. Tolkien, and* In the Shadow of Man *by Jane Goodall.*

3. *He did theater in high school! How adorable is that? Although he never took center stage, he performed in the chorus of such shows as* Anything Goes *and* West Side Story.

4. *He's a romantic. He and his girlfriend, Emma Wilson, have been together over three years! Just a few months ago, he surprised her with a trip to the Florida Keys for their anniversary!*

5. *He can't cook. A self-described novice in the kitchen, Zach rarely attempts anything more complicated than mac and cheese. But you know what? We bet that mac and cheese is as delicious as he is!*

6. *He loves to work out... and he's got the body to prove it! Let's be real. The future brother-in-law of the Prince of San Cecilio is CUT. Just check out these shirtless pictures from his Instagram!*

7. *He suffers from coulrophobia. Big time. The man who has delivered baby lion cubs and operated on Nile crocodiles is deathly afraid... of clowns. Although we don't know the specifics, we're going to go ahead and blame this one on Stephen King.*

8. *He loves girls who are smart. As if this guy couldn't get any dreamier, he is definitely one to admire a woman's intellect above her looks. Of course, with his gorgeous marketing manager girlfriend, Emma, he gets the best of both worlds!*

9. *When he was growing up, he was into dinosaurs and Greek Mythology. Fitting, for a man who looks like he belongs on Mount Olympus, himself!*

10. *Like most older brothers, he is very supportive and very protective of his little sister, and we seriously doubt her becoming a Princess will change that!*

All these reports are rather old. Still, I'm surprised I managed to miss them. I'm even more surprised by how the American media practically made Zach a celebrity just because his sister is getting married. If these articles are any indication, he's more famous than most of the royals I know, myself included. And if their content is accurate, that means that Zach was, at one point, very serious about this Emma Wilson.

I wonder what happened.

I don't believe for an instant what Lord Weston insinuated earlier; that Zach would break up with someone he cared about because he thought he could do better. At least... I don't think I do. After all, I barely know him. He may very well be just as conceited and ambitious as Weston would have me believe.

Somehow, though, I don't think he is.

CHAPTER EIGHT

Early the next morning, I return to Princess lessons with Brittany and Isabel. This week, we've been discussing social media, online presence, and how to answer when someone asks for a picture or for an autograph. The rules are really quite simple. Royals aren't allowed any of these things. No Facebook pages. No Twitter accounts. And under no circumstances are we ever permitted to sign autographs or pose for pictures.

Brittany, to no one's surprise, is not a fan of these rules.

"What's so wrong with being personable?" she asks. "I mean, I can sort of understand the no social media thing. It can be dangerous and people can use it against us or whatever. But why can't we take pictures?"

"Because it is not dignified," Princess Isabel answers. "We are not entertainers. We represent the sovereignty of San Cecilio and it is for that reason that we must hold ourselves to such standards."

"I get that, but there must be a way to connect with the people... to show them that we really care."

"And I love that you think that way, my dear. But it isn't our job to be their friends. It is our job to govern; to care for them, to keep them safe."

Brittany seems to accept this answer, even if she isn't fully convinced.

"What do *you* think about these personal policies?" she asks me after the lesson ends.

"I guess I've really never given them very much thought," I answer honestly. "Of course, I grew up with these guidelines, so I've never really questioned them."

"God, this really is a different world, isn't it?" she asks. "I mean, I'm so used to sharing my life. To talking with people and being able to let them know that I'm interested in them."

"There are lots of ways to let them know you're interested without posing for pictures or posting about it on the Internet. And I promise you'll have plenty of opportunities."

"Still. I won't really be allowed to be me, will I? I'll be a representative of the Crown."

"You're not having second thoughts, are you?"

"No, of course not. I love Nick with all my heart. This is just... a huge adjustment. Especially when so many of these rules and regulations really don't seem like that big a deal to me," she sighs. Then she shakes her head and laughs. "Oh my God, will you just listen to me? I'm about to marry the love of my life, a Prince, and I'm sitting here feeling sorry for myself."

"We're all allowed a pity party every once in a while." I think this is the first real conversation Brittany and I have ever had, and I'm surprised to find that beneath the quirks and American perkiness, there's a very genuine and thoughtful person. And you know, I think I might like her.

"Well, no more! It's almost Christmas, it's a beautiful day, and my family just flew halfway around the world to be here. I'm going to go celebrate with them. Maybe take them on a tour of the castle."

"I'm sure they'd love that," I tell her. "I think I'm going to sit and read for a bit."

"Girl, go for it," Brittany smiles at me before flouncing out of the room.

May I just say that that is the first time anyone has ever called me "Girl" in my life. And I very much hope it will be the last.

I spend the better part of the morning and early afternoon curled up under a blanket in the sitting room, sipping at spiced cider, and reading *The Giver* while the snow falls outside my window. I'm in the final few chapters when the door opens and, to my heart's utter delight, Zach appears.

"Oh, I'm sorry. I thought Britt might be in here."

"No, just me," I answer. "Did you enjoy your tour of the castle?"

"There are a lot of stairs."

I think I surprise both of us by laughing out loud.

"Yes, castles have a few."

He smiles, too. Then he notices the book in my lap.

"Are you reading *The Giver*?" he asks, his eyes lighting up.

"I am."

"And?"

"I understand why you and many of my friends speak so highly of it."

"I'm glad you're enjoying it," he says. "Sorry, by the way, for just barging in. I didn't mean to interrupt you."

"Oh, no, you didn't. I mean, it's fine. I mean..." Dear God, what is happening? It's not at all like me to get tongue-tied. "I was actually just thinking I might go for a walk." No, I absolutely was not. Why did I just tell him that?

"Would you like some company?"

"I'd love some."

Hastily, I fetch my coat, scarf, and gloves before meeting back up with Zach in the foyer.

"So, where would you like to go?" he asks me.

"Did Brittany happen to show you the gardens?"

"No, actually. Our mom was tired and wanted to rest her feet, and as much as Britt loves the snow, she has about as much tolerance for freezing temperatures as a desert tortoise."

I'm not sure I know what a desert tortoise is.

"Is that a zoo joke?"

"Sort of," he grins, stepping aside to let me lead the way out into the gardens.

Although there are no flowers in bloom beneath the frost, the majestic grounds of the castle are still a wintry wonder to behold. The bare trees are alight with white Christmas lights and the glow of sparkling snow, and the finest of ice crystals dance upon the water in every fountain.

"So I'm going to go out on a limb here and guess that your boyfriend doesn't like me very much," Zach comments casually. I don't have to ask who he means.

"He's not my boyfriend."

"No?"

"No. If he were, I never would have kissed you."

"Well, that's good," he teases.

"And I hope that you would not have agreed to kiss me back if *you* were involved with someone."

"I would not have."

"So, you don't have a girlfriend?"

"No, I don't."

"But you did."

He nods.

"We broke up about three months after Britt and Nicolás got engaged. But I promise you it was not so I could pursue 'nobler prospects.' If anything, I was hoping to distance myself from the royal spotlight. But it turned out Emma had other plans."

"Such as?"

"I should probably preface this by saying we had always been very different people. She preferred the finer things in life; things I would never be able to afford with a vet's salary. Still, I did what I could to make her happy and for the most part, we were very happy. But then, Britt met Nicolás... and Emma became obsessed."

"With what?"

"With everything. With Nicolás. With San Cecilio. With the idea that if she married me, she'd be a royal-in-law... practically a Princess."

"America seems to have an odd fixation with us," I comment. "Is it because you're a republic?"

"Probably. Though, in Emma's case, I think it had more to do with Disney," Zach admits.

"Oh, I do love *Hercules*."

"Well, so do I, but that's kind of beside the point," Zach laughs.

"I'm sorry. Please, continue."

"To make a long story short, Emma began to thrive on the attention that Britt was receiving, and it wasn't long before she started craving that same attention herself. She began telling anyone and everyone who would listen that she was dating Brittany Walker's brother... that she'd be a guest of honour at the royal wedding... Eventually, she started talking to reporters about us, about our personal lives. That was it for me."

"I'm so sorry," I tell him. "If it's any consolation, I know how you feel. I've never been one for life in the limelight. And for the most part, I've managed to avoid it. Of course, that all changed when Nicolás broke off the betrothal."

"I guess that's when life changed for both of us," Zach says.

"It was bad enough that the entire world was talking about the end of my engagement. But then they tried to paint me as the antagonist; the spoiled, selfish Princess jealous of the sweet, innocent girl who stole her Prince. They fabricated all sorts of drama and turmoil just to keep the story interesting. As if a commoner marrying into a royal family isn't interesting enough."

"Well, it has been done before," Zach reminds me with a grin. "Do you mind if I ask you a personal question?"

"I suppose that depends on what it is."

"Were you sad? You know... when he ended it?"

"I don't know if sad is the right word," I answer, trying my best to recall how I felt after receiving the phone call. "I was definitely surprised.

I didn't even know that Nicolás had met someone. Then he's calling me up, out of the blue, and telling me that he's getting married."

"Britt sort of did the same thing to us. I mean, we knew, of course, that she'd met Nicolás, and we knew that he was a Prince. But they hadn't been together very long at all when she told us that he'd asked her to marry him."

"Were your parents pleased?"

"Well, sure, they were happy for her. But it took them a while to really grasp the idea of their daughter leaving behind everything and everyone she's ever known for a man she'd only met six months earlier."

"It's sort of funny. It was the exact opposite for my parents."

"Oh, yeah?"

"They had everything sorted and settled for my future. Now that those plans have fallen through, they don't really know what to do with me. To be honest, I don't really know what to do with myself. I'm afraid my options are rather limited."

"Really? I'd have thought you could do just about anything."

"If only." Even though I'll never be Queen, as a member of the royal family, there are still rules and regulations by which I am obligated to abide.

"What *would* you do? If you could?"

"I don't know, really," I answer. "I know that I love to travel; to experience new places, new cultures. I'm also very fond of the arts, especially musicals."

"Have you ever been to New York?"

"I haven't, actually. I've only been to the United States once, and that was when I was very young. My parents were invited to attend a dinner in Washington, D.C., so they brought my brother and me along."

"Well, if you ever make it back across the pond, call me up and I'll take you to New York. Because I honestly think you would love it."

His invitation reminds me of Weston's request that I join him in London sometime. Somehow, though, Zach's casual offer feels far more genuine. He's not trying to show off or impress me. He simply thinks I would enjoy it.

Smiling up at him, I reply, "You know, I might just do that."

CHAPTER NINE

The Walkers have been here almost three days now and finally, we're taking them into Valoña for a history tour, followed by an afternoon of holiday festivities. And by "we," I mean Nicolás, Brittany, Weston, and I.

First, we visit the home of David Emilio Marques, the famous eighteenth-century poet. Then we stop by the National Art and Sculpture Gallery, followed by lunch at a local cafe. Naturally, we're met at each location by a small army of photographers, but thanks to our security staff, they keep their distance.

"I wonder what the press will make of you and me," Weston muses softly in my ear.

Oh, I can only imagine.

"You know, Weston, as much as I enjoy your company, I must tell you I'm not really looking to rush into anything."

"Oh, no, I absolutely agree! There's no rush at all. I'm sorry, I didn't mean to imply that we... I mean, that you and I... All I meant, really, was that there are bound to be pictures of us together and, well, I'm sure there will be those in the media who will draw their own conclusions..." Weston rambles as our waiter returns with our drinks and tapas.

"I don't doubt it." Especially if any of those cameras happened to catch us engaging in what must look like a very intimate conversation.

After lunch, we make our way downtown to visit the shops and to get a taste of a true San Cecilian Christmas. Every business, it turns out, has their own way of celebrating the season. For example, the pharmacy has constructed a massive toy village around a collection of working model trains. The post office has a tree decorated entirely with handwritten notes and old photographs. But my favourite by far is the Christmas cookie decorating station in the bakery.

Our last stop for the day is the *Catedral de Santa Catalina*, or the Cathedral of Saint Catherine. It's one of the oldest Cathedrals still standing on the Iberian Peninsula and San Cecilio's most revered landmark. It's not nearly as grand as Santiago de Compostela or as famous as Notre Dame, but it's a glorious building nevertheless.

"Now, is this where they have the parade every year?" Mr. Walker asks.

"What parade?" Zach asks.

"You don't know about *El Desfile de Estrellas*? The Parade of Stars?" Brittany asks her brother. "Oh my God, it's magical."

"It is actually a very sacred tradition," Nicolás explains. "On Christmas Eve, every observing citizen gathers in the street leading to Santa Catalina for a procession of Christmas stars, hand-crafted by local artists, business owners, even students. There's no fee, no application. If you have a star, you are welcome to march. Once the parade has passed, the viewers follow the stars into the Cathedral for Midnight Mass. It is our way of welcoming the Christ Child and inviting those from far and wide to join us at His manger."

"That's lovely," Mrs. Walker says.

Suddenly, Brittany gasps.

"That's it," she says.

"What's it?" Zach asks.

To my surprise, she turns to me.

"Rosalind, do you remember the conversation we had earlier this week? About, you know, personal policies and really connecting with the people?"

"Yes..."

"Well, I have an idea. And as far as I know, it doesn't violate any sort of royal protocol!" she exclaims. "What if we made our own stars and walked in the parade?"

"Has that ever been done before?" I ask.

"Not as far as I know," Nicolás answers.

"So, what do you think? It is a good idea?" Brittany wants to know.

"It is a beautiful idea, my love," Nicolás tells her. "However..."

"What?"

"I know our personal policies and royal protocol seem a little silly to you. And I understand. But you see, we are not supposed to be the focus of *El Desfile de Estrellas*, and if we were to participate, it may distract from what the night is really supposed to be about."

"But you always attend."

"True, but we stay in the background. We don't take center stage."

"Then we don't have to march. But I still think we should make our own stars," Brittany says.

"Perhaps we could donate them," I suggest. "I'm sure there are those out there who would love to participate but have neither the time nor the resources to build a star."

"Oh my God, that's an amazing idea!" Brittany declares. "Okay, as soon as we get home, I am going to make a list of all the supplies we'll need. Oh, and I need to know how many of you want to help and if you want to construct your own star or if you'd like to buddy up with someone. Then, if you want, we can have a meeting tonight after dinner to discuss ideas, maybe sketch out some designs..."

"Sweetheart," Mrs. Walker chimes in. "I love that you're so excited about this, but are you going to have time to do all this? Remember, the wedding is only a week away."

"Actually, it's nine days. That gives us plenty of time!" Brittany insists before looking back to us. "What do you guys say?"

"I say yes, as I always will to you," Nicolás tells her.

"I'm in," Zach agrees.

"So am I," I say.

"I'm not sure I'll know what I'm doing, but count me in," Weston says.

Brittany bounces and squeals with delight.

"Oh my God, you guys are the best! This is going to be so much fun! And we can totally watch Christmas movies to inspire us while we work!"

"She never runs out of energy, does she?" I mutter to Zach.

"Never has, never will," he answers with a fond smile.

And in that moment, I can't help myself. I smile too.

As soon as we arrive back at the castle, Brittany immediately sprints inside to get to work on her Christmas Star passion. Her parents, Nicolás, and Weston follow closely behind, but Zach and I linger back, walking slowly along the snow-covered path.

"Today was fun," he says.

"It was," I agree.

"I've got to tell you, I had a lot of reservations about coming here."

"To San Cecilio?"

"To the castle. I wasn't sure if I could keep up with the royal lifestyle."

"It can be overwhelming. But if I may say so, you're getting along splendidly."

"Thanks. I'm trying."

"You're succeeding."

We wander a few steps further in silence before he says, "You know, I couldn't help but overhear that talk you had with Lord Weston over lunch."

"Oh? Which one?"

"The one where you told him you weren't looking to rush into anything," he reminds me, looking awfully smug.

"Oh, right. That one."

"He seemed to take it okay."

"He may be a little overly optimistic."

"Well, you can't blame a guy for hoping," he comments. Then, with a cheeky grin, he asks, "Does he know you kissed me?"

I'm caught so off guard by his impertinence that I laugh aloud.

"Absolutely not!" I answer.

"Have you ever kissed him?"

Again, I'm scandalized.

"I don't think these questions are at all appropriate." I'm trying to scold him but it is not having the desired effect. He is enjoying this far too much.

"But you were the one who asked to kiss me!"

"Yes. I remember."

"I'm just saying... kissing strangers on street corners doesn't seem very dignified to me."

All right. That does it.

"Oh, you want dignified, do you, Dr. Walker?"

"It's what I've been told to expect."

So, without skipping a beat, I kneel down, scoop up a handful of snow, and toss it playfully in his direction. The stunned look on his face is everything I could have hoped for and more.

"Oh, you're in trouble," he warns, reaching down to collect his own snow.

"No!" I squeal and dart off into the gardens.

Unfortunately, he is much faster than I am and catches up with me in moments. Everything is an icy blur as I do my best to evade him, all the while gathering my snowy ammunition.

By the time the war is over, I'm shivering, soaked to the bone, and laughing so hard I can barely catch my breath. Zach is in a similar state of delight and distress.

"Okay, you win, you win," he pants. "I surrender, Your Highness."

"You fought with honour. I think we can call it a truce," I tell him.

"How gracious of you."

73

"I'm a diplomat at heart."

"As a good ruler must be."

"Oh, I'm never going to rule anything." I mean it as an offhanded remark, but Zach looks rather taken aback, almost like he thinks he may have offended me. Which, of course, he hasn't. Still, I'm afraid I've dispelled the magic of our wonderful afternoon.

"I'm sorry. That was stupid of me," he apologizes. "I didn't mean - "

"No, please. You have no reason to be sorry. It's just a fact," I assure him. "Now, come on. Let's go and get warm. Then, maybe, Brittany will be so good as to share with us all of her ideas for our Christmas stars."

CHAPTER TEN

The day following our adventures in San Cecilio begins, as usual, with Princess lessons, followed immediately by our first aptly named Star Session. By the time I arrive with Nicolás, Weston, and Zach, Brittany has already converted the green drawing room into an art studio, complete with folding work tables, construction paper, paint, wire, glue, glitter, and a dozen and a half other supplies.

"Wow, Britt. This looks amazing," Zach tells her.

"You... managed to do this all in one day?" Weston asks.

"Well, I mean, being engaged to the Prince does have *some* perks," Brittany grins.

"So, how do we actually go about this?" Weston wants to know.

"However you want! From what I understand, the star can be as large or as small as you like. It can be made from most materials, as long as it can't be used as a weapon. For example, the butcher can't make a star out of knives."

"Well, there goes my idea," Zach jokes.

As we set to work, I grab a few pieces of white construction paper and a pencil. I have an idea for what I want my star to be, but first, I need to be able to visualize it. Zach, Nicolás, and Brittany, however, are all ready and set to begin construction.

I've just finished sketching out my idea when I hear Brittany ask, "Zach, what are those?"

"What are what?" he responds.

"Those red and blue sticks. And why... why is your star just... a circle?"

"Because my star isn't just any star. My star... is the Death Star." He grins, holding up his masterpiece.

"The *what*?" I ask.

"Are you *kidding* me?" Brittany demands.

Nicolás, meanwhile, throws his head back and laughs.

"Oh, that is *brilliant*!" He exclaims.

"No it isn't!" Brittany scolds. "These stars represent the holiest night of the year! You can't donate the Death Star! It's evil!"

"What if I make a little Christmas tree out of light sabers?" Zach asks, holding up the red and blue sticks.

"Oh! You could throw in some tiny Ewoks dressed as the Three Kings!" Nicolás grins.

"No!" Brittany declares yet again.

Meanwhile, I am completely lost.

"I feel like you're all speaking a foreign language," I tell them.

"Wait a minute. You've never seen *Star Wars*?" Zach is suddenly staring at me with a strange mixture of pity and concern.

"No. I've heard of it, of course. But I'm not exactly versed in its... vocabulary."

"That's okay," Brittany assures me.

Zach, on the other hand, does not seem to agree with her.

"Rose, Rose," he sighs, sounding as though I've physically pained him. "I thought you were cool."

"*Rose*?" Weston asks, raising a curious eyebrow.

"Yeah, Wes. It's a nickname," Zach explains.

"I'm aware. I just don't think I've ever heard anyone address a Princess so informally."

"What's the big deal? I call Nicolás Nick," Brittany reminds him.

"Yes, well, you're engaged to him. It's different," Weston argues.

"I don't know. I rather like it," I say.

"I do, too," Brittany agrees. "Besides, it's not like this is a formal setting. We're all friends."

"Yes, I suppose little things like *status* don't really matter at the arts and crafts table," Weston remarks with a glance at Zach that both challenges and disparages. Zach, of course, doesn't seem at all threatened by Weston or his snide comment.

As the minutes tick by, I become more and more aware of Weston's eyes flitting back and forth between Zach and me, and the longer I'm under his gaze, the more self-conscious I become.

I think he knows. And if he doesn't know, then he at least suspects. Not that there's anything to suspect. Not really. Zach is a friend. A very handsome friend. But still, just a friend.

When the time comes to dress for dinner, we abandon our stars and disperse throughout the castle to our respective suites and bedrooms. Sophie, of course, is waiting for me with a stylishly simple blue dress with a beaded neckline.

"Did you enjoy your afternoon, Your Highness?" she asks me.

"I did," I answer. "I'm afraid my star may be a little... lopsided. But it's pink and gold and very glittery, so I hope that makes up for it."

"Well, I think it's a wonderful thing you're all doing. In fact, I'm thinking of making a star myself."

"You should!" I exclaim. "Come down to the drawing room with me tomorrow."

"Are you sure?"

"Absolutely. We'd all be delighted. And we have plenty of supplies. Miss Walker made sure of that."

"Thank you, Your Highness," Sophie grins.

I've just finished applying a light touch of lip gloss when someone knocks on my door.

"Yes, come in," I call.

The door opens and my heart leaps into my throat when I see Zach standing in the hallway. Even Sophie blushes.

"Oh... hello," I greet him. "If it isn't the Lord of the *Star Wars*."

"Is that like... *The Lord of the Rings*?" he asks.

"You know, I actually *have* seen that," I tell him.

"And I'm very proud of you," he teases. Then he notices Sophie standing behind me and extends his hand. "Hey, I'm Zach."

"Hello," Sophie giggles. In all the years I've known her, I have never seen her in such a tizzy.

"Er... Zach, this is my lady-in-waiting, Sophie."

"It's nice to meet you," Zach smiles.

"You as well, Sir," Sophie squeaks.

"Zach is Miss Walker's brother," I explain.

"Oh, yes, of course. I've heard of you," she says. "I mean... not directly, of course. I just... I knew you were here with your family. And I knew Miss Walker had a brother. But I never knew your name." Finally, Sophie catches herself. "Forgive me, I think I'm rambling."

"It's fine," Zach assures her.

"Well, er... it was lovely to meet you, but I really must see to something... Excuse me." Then, with a quick, clumsy curtsy, she flees and disappears into her adjoining bedroom.

"Is she going to be okay?" Zach asks, trying and failing to hide his amusement.

"Oh, of course," I answer. "This is just... her first time meeting an American."

"Ah. Well, I hope she wasn't disappointed."

"I don't think she was."

"So you don't think she'd mind too terribly if I asked you to watch a movie with me tonight?"

"You mean... just you and me?" I ask, my pulse fluttering in my throat.

"Yeah."

"Is it *Star Wars*?"

"Sadly, it is not. I had to raid my sister's collection and her taste in movies is mediocre at best."

"So you're asking me on a mediocre movie date?"

"Oh no, this particular movie is fantastic."

"Well, that's good to know."

"So... will you come?"

"I'd love to," I tell him.

"Great," he grins. "Oh, and just so you know, the dress code is cozy and very casual."

79

"I've done casual before."

He laughs. I love the sound of his laughter. And I love that I'm the one making him laugh.

"Okay, good. So we won't have to make a midnight Walmart run."

"What's a Walmart?"

"I wouldn't even know where to begin," he answers. "So, uh... I guess I'll see you downstairs."

"Actually I'm ready to go now if you'd care to escort me."

"It would be my pleasure, Your Highness," he says, offering me his arm.

"You know, I think I prefer it when you call me Rose."

He smiles down at me as if to share a secret.

"I think I do, too."

After a comforting and filling feast of grilled vegetables, soup, and pasta, I slip back up to my bedroom to brush my teeth and, as requested, to change into more casual attire. Sophie is still at dinner with the rest of the staff, so I'm not going to interrupt her. I'm perfectly capable of picking out my own clothes. Besides, I know she's going to interrogate me about Zach the second she gets me alone and I don't know how much I'm ready to share with her.

Once I've changed into my blue jeans and large, cozy jumper, I make my way down to the green drawing room where Zach is already waiting. Even dressed in old blue jeans and a simple button-down shirt, he looks every bit the handsome Prince.

"Come in," he beckons me. "I'm trying to decide if I should risk moving the couch a little closer. I don't want to disturb the stars."

I'm halfway to thinking that's oddly poetic of him until I realize he's referencing the stars that we're making, not the ones that shape our destinies.

"I think you'll be fine," I tell him. "Do you want some help?"

"Am I allowed to let you help?" he asks playfully.

At that, I roll my eyes.

"For Heaven's sake, I'm not a withering orchid."

"But you are a Rose," he reminds me.

"That joke is dreadful."

"Fair."

Together, we manage to move the sofa in between our crafts tables and the television. It's a little crowded, but somehow, it feels very warm and welcoming. In fact, I'm tempted to say that it feels a little like home.

"So, what are we watching?" I ask Zach once I've chosen my spot on the sofa.

"Well, I know you love musicals, so I thought you might enjoy this." He hands me a movie case depicting a circus-type setting, a dark-haired ringmaster, and a dozen vibrant colours.

"*The Greatest Showman*," I read aloud.

"Have you seen it?"

"No, but I've heard wonderful things."

"Trust me, what you've heard doesn't do it justice."

"I daresay you've got me intrigued, Dr. Walker," I tell him. "Let's see it, then."

And so we watch it, and it's everything that Zach promised and more. From the opening number to the last sentimental scene, I find myself utterly transfixed by the music, the cinematography, and the passion of every actor and artist involved. I'm so mesmerized by the movie that I don't realize that I've managed to nestle into Zach's warm embrace until the credits begin to roll.

"So, what did you think?" he asks, grinning down at me.

"I think I'm going to try to convince my father to invite the entire cast to the palace for New Year's Eve," I answer.

"You really liked it?"

"I loved it."

"Good. I'm glad," he says, shifting his body so that I'm pressed even closer to him. I wonder if he notices. "Do you mind if I ask you something?"

"Not at all."

"What's it like? Growing up in a place like this? Living... this kind of life?"

"You mean... royal?"

"Yeah."

"It's difficult to say, really, because it's the only life I've ever known. To me, growing up in a palace was and still is perfectly ordinary. It's grand, it's spacious, but at the same time, that space is always full of people. Whether they be courtiers or members of the staff or tourists on vacation, the palace is never empty. It's almost impossible to find a moment's peace or time just to myself..." Oh, my goodness. Listen to me. I'm complaining. I'm actually complaining about my life of wealth and privilege. "But really, it was wonderful. It is

82

wonderful. And of course, Mondovia is the most beautiful place in the world. I love it with all my heart."

"I'd love to see it," Zach says, his voice soft and low.

"Maybe one day you will," I whisper, my mouth mere inches from his.

Just then, the clock on the wall begins to chime, startling both of us. It strikes twelve times before falling silent.

"Do you think our Fairy Godmothers will be upset with us for staying up past midnight?" Zach asks me.

"Well, I can't speak for yours, but mine is very understanding," I tell him. "She even let me keep the glass slippers."

"Hmm. Mine didn't fit," he jokes.

"Oh, now that is sad," I giggle.

"It's fine. They're not very practical footwear for a veterinarian."

"Is that what you've always wanted to do? Work with animals?"

"Yes and no," he answers. "I have always wanted to work with animals, but I didn't decide to pursue a career in veterinary medicine until college. I told you the day we met that my dream was to go on safari in Africa, but that's just a small part of what I really want to do."

"And what's that?"

"I want to work in wildlife conservation, to be a sort of ambassador if you will. I want to help fight trophy-hunting and illegal poaching. I want to give endangered species their futures back."

"Then do it," I tell him.

"I'd love to. But I'm not really sure where to begin."

"I'm not sure if you're aware of this, Zachary, but life has just dealt you an extraordinary hand. One that is rather hard to beat." He looks at me, expecting me to elaborate. "Your sister's engagement to Nicolás has already catapulted you into the public eye. I know it isn't what you expected, or what you wanted, but you could easily use your new status to your advantage."

"I guess I never really thought of that. I mean, she's the one marrying the Prince. I'm just the guy who shares her parents."

"Well, take it from someone who grew up as 'the spare.' You don't have to be a sovereign to make an impact. You're going to have a lot of influence as the Princess of San Cecilio's brother. You already do."

"Thank you," he says, sounding absolutely sincere.

"Don't mention it. To tell you the truth, it's something I could stand to remind myself every now and then," I admit. "I'm afraid I've struggled with... clarity this year."

"I can understand that. I mean... Britt wasn't the only one whose life changed when she said yes to Nicolás."

"That's very true. But you know, I really am very glad she did." *Because if she hadn't, I never would have met you.* Even though I don't say the words aloud, he seems to sense them.

"I am, too," he agrees.

And then, ever so softly, ever so gently, he kisses me.

CHAPTER ELEVEN

My heart is still dancing when I open my eyes the following morning. I'm not exactly sure what I'm feeling, but I am very certain that I've never felt like this before. I'm certain that the world has never been like this before. The sun has never shone so brightly. The air has never smelled so sweet. Everything is beautiful and wonderful and new.

I dress quickly, eager to begin the day... and eager to see Zach again. It's barely been seven hours and yet, it feels like an eternity has passed since we were last together.

Since he kissed me.

Oh, my God. Zach kissed me. And it was magic. It was as though we'd never kissed before. And perhaps, in a way, we really hadn't. Our first kiss was no more than a fleeting moment between strangers... strangers who had no intention of ever seeing the other again.

The kiss we shared last night was entirely different.

With one last look in the mirror to make sure my hair and makeup are flawless, I flounce out of my room and scamper to the grand staircase where, to my surprise, I meet Lord Weston.

"Good morning, Weston," I greet him.

"Good morning, *Rose*," he responds. "I trust you had a pleasant evening?"

"It was lovely. Thank you."

"No doubt Dr. Walker enjoyed himself as well."

How does he know...?

Never mind. It doesn't matter. And it certainly isn't any of his business.

"Yes, well - "

"You need to be careful with him," Weston interrupts. I'll admit I'm taken aback by his sudden outburst.

"I'm sorry?"

"No, no. I'm sorry. I didn't mean to sound like I'm scolding you."

"Good."

I try to move past him, then, but he stops me.

"The truth is that I don't trust him," he says, all in a rush. "And I don't think you should either."

"Do you even know him?"

"That's not the point."

"What is, then?"

"What all has he told you about his girlfriend?"

"That they're broken up for starters."

"Did he mention that before she was his girlfriend, she was one of Brittany's best friends? And that they stayed friends after the break-up?"

"No, but that's not really my concern."

"So it's not your concern either, then, that she'll be flying in for the wedding in just a few days... or that Britt and Nicolás have invited her to stay here at the castle." It's then and only then that I waver in my resolve to not let him get to me. And he knows it, too. He can see the shadow of doubt he's cast in my mind. "Why do you suppose he didn't tell you?"

"Perhaps he was going to and you beat him to it," I suggest, having recovered quickly from my momentary lapse in composure. "Now, if you've nothing more to say, I do hope you'll excuse me. I'm famished."

Breakfast is an informal affair. Zach doesn't even show up. I suspect he's sleeping in, as he's done a few times before. I'm sure he'll be down by the time Princess lessons are over. This morning, we're discussing wedding etiquette. It's really very much the same as banquet and ballroom etiquette. But it will be Brittany's first appearance as an official member of the royal family, and she'll be surrounded by dozens of her American friends who, undoubtedly, will not be familiar with royal protocol.

"It will be expected of you to greet every guest, but be careful not to show favour to any guest in particular. Be gracious, but keep the conversations light. And remember, no photographs," Princess Isabel instructs.

"Got it," Brittany says.

"You know, when your friends arrive, it might be nice for them to sit in on a few of these lessons."

"Oh, my God, they would actually love that," Brittany tells her. "My friend, Emma especially. She has literally *always* wanted to be a Princess."

Emma. That's her. Zach's former girlfriend.

Lord Weston was right.

Not that I ever suspected him of being untruthful. But I had hoped that he had been misinformed.

"Well, I hope we do not disappoint her," Princess Isabel laughs.

"Believe me. That would be impossible," Brittany says. "Oh! And good news! I've talked to her, Ashley, and Amanda and they're all going to make their very own stars for the parade! Isn't that exciting?"

"Sophie was hoping she might make one as well," I announce. "My lady-in-waiting?"

"Yeah, for sure! This is a project for everyone," Brittany says. "Invite her to our session this morning!"

"Actually, I already have."

"Perfect!"

"I must tell you I think this is wonderful, what you are doing," Princess Isabel says. "A very thoughtful gift for the people of San Cecilio."

"Thank you, Your Highness," Brittany smiles.

"You are welcome, my dear. Now, I believe we are done for the day."

"Great!" Brittany exclaims. "Rosalind, go get Sophie! I'll grab the boys and meet you in the drawing room."

I do as she says and sure enough, when we arrive, all of them, including Zach, are there waiting. His face lights up the moment he sees me. I'm so dazzled by his smile that, for half a moment, I forget all about Emma.

"This is all so very exciting!" Sophie exclaims, taking her place at the crafts table. "I've always wanted to see *El Desfile de Estrellas*. Now, to actually get to participate in such a historic and holy tradition... It's like a dream come true!"

"I love your enthusiasm, Sophie," Nicolás grins at her.

"Thank you, Your Highness."

"Call me Nicolás," he tells her.

"Oh, no. I don't think I can do that," she laughs.

"Sure you can. It's easy."

"There are no formalities in this room," Weston comments in a stuck-up, disgruntled tone.

"You sound like you don't approve, Wes," Zach remarks.

"Yes, well, we all know how much respect *you* have for royalty, Dr. Walker," Weston bites back.

"What's that supposed to mean?" Brittany asks.

"Nothing," Weston mutters. "You must be looking forward to seeing your friends, Britt. When are they arriving, again?"

"Ashley and Amanda won't be here until the night before the wedding but Emma is flying in the day after tomorrow!"

Suddenly, the smile fades from Zach's face and for the first time since I've known him, he looks genuinely troubled.

"You didn't tell me that," he says.

"You knew she was coming to the wedding," Brittany reminds him.

"Yeah, but I thought - " he stops mid-sentence when he catches me staring. "I didn't realize she'd be here so long."

"What do you expect? She's my best friend. Besides, she's really looking forward to seeing you again."

"Perhaps you will be able to rekindle an old spark," Nicolás grins.

That's it. I can't listen to this. I know exactly how it will look if I leave, but I don't care. Setting my half-finished star aside, I rise quickly, startling my fellow craftsmen.

"Rosalind, are you all right?" Brittany asks, looking panicked.

"Yes, yes, I'm fine. Just a bit of a headache, that's all. Please excuse me," I answer. Then, before anyone can question me further, I dash out into the hallway.

I'm halfway to the foyer when I hear a voice calling my name. His voice.

"Rose!"

And of course, I stop and turn to face him.

"I am so sorry," Zach breathes once he catches up to me.

"You've no need to apologize," I tell him.

"Yes, I have. I should have told you that Emma was coming, I just... I had really been hoping that I wouldn't have to spend that much time with her, if any."

"She's your sister's closest friend and a woman you loved for three years. How, exactly, were you planning to avoid her?" I'm not asking to be rude. I'm genuinely curious. From where I'm standing, his logic is tragically flawed.

"It's a big wedding," he answers simply.

"Oh, how you underestimate the determination of women. Especially women in love."

"She's not in love with me," he says. "But even if she still were, it wouldn't matter. It's over between us. It's been over between us for months."

He sounds adamant, but something remains unclear to me.

"May I ask you a personal question?"

"Anything," he tells me.

"You told me that you broke up with her because she was talking to the media about you. If that's so... why did Brittany stay friends with her?"

Zach takes a deep breath.

"Because I didn't tell her," he answers.

"Why not?"

"Because I didn't want to come between them. Britt and Emma have been friends since their freshman year of college. But it wasn't only that," he admits. "Britt has this gift. She only ever sees the good in people. Growing up, I thought it made her vulnerable, but the older I get, the more I understand just how lucky she is. I don't want her to see the side of Emma that I saw, especially on the happiest day of her life."

"That's so noble of you," I tell him.

He shrugs.

"She's my little sister. I'd do anything to protect her."

"That's how I feel about my brother," I tell him. "Even though he's older, I've always felt like he's the one that needs protecting. Probably because he has so much responsibility as heir. At times, I really think it overwhelms him."

"As it would anyone," Zach says.

"May I ask you another personal question?"

"Go for it."

"Why does Brittany think your relationship with Emma ended?"

"I told her it was just one of those things. We had different priorities, different goals. Emma tried her best to make me seem like the villain of the piece, but she couldn't tell Britt the real reason she was so upset with me without exposing herself."

"Do you suppose that she does... want you back?"

"She might," he answers honestly. "But like I said before, it doesn't matter. I wouldn't go back to her. Besides..." he says, taking both of my hands in his. "I kind of like someone else."

"Oh?" I ask, my heart skipping several beats. "Anyone I know?"

"Just this smart, beautiful, crazy amazing girl I met in a bookshop. She hasn't seen *Star Wars* though, so I don't know if it's going to work out - "

"Shut it!" I laugh, throwing my arms around his strong, sturdy shoulders.

"On a totally unrelated note... I know what I'm getting you for Christmas."

"Hmm... I wonder what it could be?" I tease.

Then, there in the middle of the hall, where anyone could catch us at any moment, I lean forward and press my lips to his.

CHAPTER TWELVE

A fierce and unforgiving snowstorm moves into Valoña the day that Emma arrives in San Cecilio. Although Mondovia sees its fair share of snowfall and withstands several thunderstorms a year, I'm not at all accustomed to squalls of this magnitude. It's rather unnerving.

Fortunately, Emma's plane lands safely mere moments before the airport announced it was grounding all remaining flights. Unfortunately, due to hazardous travel conditions, it takes the driver that Britt and Nicolás sent for her nearly three hours to navigate the roads and deliver her to the castle.

The dreadful weather does nothing to dampen anyone's spirits, however. Especially Emma's.

"Oh, my God, Britt! Just *look* at this place!"

She and Brittany are shrieking and squealing in the grand foyer but I can hear them all the way from the sitting room.

"I know! Isn't it gorgeous?"

"I could die. I could literally die. I can't believe you get to live here. This is actually like a real-life fairy tale!" Emma exclaims. Then, she asks, "So uh... where's Zach?"

Zach, it just so happens, is sitting on the sofa next to me. We've been here, wrapped in blankets, sipping hot tea, and telling each other stories from our childhoods, for hours now. It may not seem like much, but honestly, I've enjoyed this afternoon of pure simplicity as much as any extravagant outing. Possibly even more.

Now, however, Zach looks at me with wary eyes as his sister answers, "I don't know. He might be up in his room..."

"Do you want to go greet her?" I ask him.

"Do you want to go with me?"

"I will."

So, heaving an overly-exaggerated sigh, Zach lifts himself up off the sofa and offers his hand to help me up as well. As I follow him out into the foyer, I keep my head held high. Part of me wishes I could disappear into thin air. The other part, however, wishes I'd worn my new tiara for my first meeting with Miss Emma Wilson.

"Oh, there he is!" Brittany announces as soon as Zach enters the foyer.

Emma turns to look and I'm immediately struck by how gorgeous she is. She's tall, though not quite as tall as I am, and incredibly slender. Her hair is dark like mine, but perfectly straight, and her eyes are as icy blue as the frozen waters of the castle fountains.

"Zach! Oh my God!" she exclaims. Then, she runs to him and throws herself into his arms. "Oh, it is so good to see you."

"Good to see you too, Em," he says.

"Look at you! My God, you look great! And you have a beard now?"

"I've been begging him to shave it for the wedding," Brittany remarks.

"I like it," Zach argues.

"So do I," I agree, waltzing right into their little reunion. Emma's eyes look me up and down. I think she recognizes me but she can't seem to place me. "Hello, I don't believe we've met."

94

"Oh, I'm sorry!" Brittany says. "Rose, this is my best friend, Emma Wilson. Em, this is Rosalind."

"Wait, Rosalind? Like... *Princess* Rosalind?" Emma asks.

"Of Mondovia. Yes," I answer.

"But... you... aren't you the one who was supposed to marry Nick?"

"Again, yes."

"Oh. Okay." Emma casts a curious glance in Brittany's direction before turning back to me. "So like, not to be rude or anything, but why are you here?"

First of all, that *is* rather rude. Second of all, my reasons for being here are none of her business. But she's asked the question. I might as well have a bit of fun.

"To win him back and steal the throne, obviously."

Her wintery eyes widen as though she actually believes me. Brittany and Zach, on the other hand, burst out laughing.

"Rosalind and Nick have been friends for years," Brittany explains. "His family is practically her family."

"And you're seriously okay with her being here?" Emma asks before quickly adding, "No offense."

"Absolutely!" Brittany answers. "I love Rose!"

She does? Aw, that is sweet, isn't it?

"Thank you, Brittany. I'm very fond of you as well," I tell her. She beams.

But then, she opens her mouth again.

"Besides, she's found herself another suitor," she informs Emma, who looks to Zach almost immediately. Brittany must notice because she begins to laugh. "No, not him. Lord Weston!"

"The Lord Weston we met up with in London that one time?"

"Yes!"

"Oh! Okay. He's cute. And he had great taste in pretty much everything. Kudos," she tells me.

I don't know what *kudos* are, but I don't think I want them from her.

"Actually, Lord Weston and I are merely close acquaintances," I correct them.

"Don't let him hear you say that. As far as he's concerned, the two of you are going to be the next royal 'it' couple," Brittany says.

That is precisely the last thing I want. I know what it's like to have the media watching your every move. I saw the way that reporters and photographers followed and fawned over Brittany and Nicolás throughout the course of their entire romance. That may have been well and good for them, but I have no interest in making a grand production of my personal life.

Of course, if I'm hoping to pursue a romantic relationship with Zach - and in my heart, I know that I am - I'm going to have to prepare myself for the attention that is sure to follow. Because it wouldn't just be another royal dating an American commoner. Oh, no. This has the potential to become an international scandal that the media will just adore: ***Prince Nicolás's Former Betrothed is Dating his New Brother-In-Law!***

We'll just be one big happy royal family, won't we?

"Yes, well, even if I were to date Lord Weston, I'm afraid I'm not really one for the spotlight," I tell them.

Emma, to my surprise, responds with a shrill laugh and a shake of her long dark hair.

"Then you were born into the wrong occupation."

After Britt takes Emma on her introductory tour of the castle, we all reconvene in the green drawing room to show off our stars.

Brittany's is truly a reflection of the Christmas spirit. It's covered in red and green lace, adorned with gold and silver jingle bells. Nicolás's looks more like an actual star shining in the night sky. Weston's is a tribute to the city of Valoña, with its historic skyline drawn in detail against the star's gold background. Sophie's, perhaps, is the most impressive of all. Hers is crafted to resemble a stained-glass window.

Then there's mine. I fear with its simple gold structure and pink rhinestone decorations, my star is remarkably mediocre. I like it, though. I think it's pretty.

Of course, Emma only has eyes for Zach and his creation.

"Wait a minute... is that the *Death Star*?" she asks. "Oh my God, Zach, you didn't!"

"Oh, he did," Brittany grumbles.

"That is just so *you*, isn't it?" Emma sighs. "Do you remember when we went to the midnight showing of *The Force Awakens* and the movie theater threw that big Welcome Back *Star Wars* party?"

"How could I forget?" Zach asks.

"It was actually one of our first dates," Emma explains to the rest of us. "And Zach was just so excited that night. I remember these guys were there operating a couple of droids that were like, rolling around and greeting people and Zach just had to have a picture with both of them! You know, I bet I can find it..."

"Maybe some other time, Em," Zach tells her.

"Okay, fine. But they really should see it sometime because you are adorable."

Zach flashes an apologetic grimace in my direction.

"You know, we should do something fun tonight in honour of your arrival," Brittany says to Emma. "I would suggest going into town and looking at all the lights, but we're kind of snowed in."

"We could always have another movie night," Nicolás suggests.

"We could... but I want Em to really be able to get to know everyone," Brittany argues. "I've got it! What about a game night?"

"Oh, my God, that sounds like so much fun!" Emma exclaims. "Game night in a real castle!"

"And since we've got six people, we could easily break into teams of two or three," Weston observes.

"I call dibs on Zach, then," Emma announces, looping her arm through his. "We always made a pretty good team, didn't we?"

Standing there, watching them interact, I'm suddenly fully aware of just how much history they have between them. Of course, I have my history with Nicolás, but it's not nearly the same thing. Nicolás and I were paired off by our parents. We never had that relationship, that foundation of common interests and shared experiences. In many ways, Zach and Emma were much closer in their partnership than Nicolás and I ever were in ours. And I can't say why, but that makes me rather sad.

These last few days with Zach have been magical for me, but what are a few short days when compared to almost three years? Even though he insisted that whatever once existed between them is gone, it clearly isn't forgotten. By either of them.

How can I ever hope to compete with that?

CHAPTER THIRTEEN

By the time I return to my room to dress for dinner, I'm feeling glum and very homesick. I want to talk to my brother. I miss him.

Figuring I have at least twenty minutes to spare, I grab my phone off of its place on the nightstand and press the **Call** button next to his name.

He answers on the first ring.

"Rose?"

"Oh, Robert, it's so good to hear your voice."

"You sound low. Are you feeling all right?"

"I'm fine. I'm just missing home. And missing you."

"Believe me, I miss you, too. I've just endured a very meaningful conversation with Mum and Dad."

"Oh, dear." In our family, a "meaningful conversation" is one that usually involves shouting. But of course, royals don't shout. We negotiate. Loudly. "Anything I should know about?"

"I'll fill you in when I see you in a few days."

That's right! Robert and our mother are flying into Valoña on Christmas Eve! Oh, I'm so overcome with relief that I could weep!

"So," Robert continues. "Are you ready?"

"For...?"

"The wedding."

"I am, actually," I answer with complete confidence. "Nicolás and Miss Walker... they really were made for each other."

"I'm so happy to hear you say that," Robert tells me. "Not the part about Nicolás and Miss

Walker, though I am glad for them. But I am *truly* happy that you've made peace with them. And with the wedding."

"So am I."

"Could a certain Lord Weston have anything to do with that?"

"Did you *really* just ask me that?" I laugh.

"What? Am I not allowed to be curious?"

"Well, for your information, no. My change of heart has nothing to do with Lord Weston." I know that if I wanted to mention Zach to my brother, now would be the perfect moment, but something holds me back. Not that I think he would disapprove. Quite the contrary. I think he would be delighted to find out I was dating a doctor.

But the thing is I'm *not* dating a doctor. Not yet, anyway. Not officially. We haven't talked about what will happen once the wedding is over and we return to our lives in the real world. And I don't see the point in discussing him with anyone, especially my family, until we do.

Because for all I know, our first Christmas together may very well be our last.

"A balloon? A key! Is it a... very strange umbrella?"

"Time!" Brittany calls.

I turn to Lord Weston, who is clearly very confused by my admittedly mediocre artwork.

"It's an elephant," I tell him. "*Like Water for Elephants.*"

We're playing a game called Pictionary and it probably goes without saying that I am not very good at it. So far, Nicolás and Brittany are winning by a considerable margin with Zach and Emma in second and Lord Weston and me trailing at dead last. I don't care all that much about winning, though. I'm far more concerned with how closely Emma has snuggled herself up next to Zach.

"Oh, my God, I love elephants," Emma exclaims before turning to Zach. "Do you remember the time you took me to that elephant sanctuary in Oklahoma? And we got to feed them? I swear, elephants are my spirit animal."

"Have you been to the elephant orphanage in Kenya?" I ask, knowing full well that she hasn't.

"No, I haven't," she answers lightly, as though I've just challenged her. And I suppose I have.

"Oh, you must. It's a wonderful facility. The workers there are really making a difference."

"I'd love to visit it," Zach says.

"We should go!" Emma tells him. "I mean, you've been talking about going to Africa forever. We should just do it! It could be our New Year's Resolution! What do you think?"

"I... think we should just focus on getting through the next few days before making any new plans," Zach answers. Very diplomatically, I might add.

Emma's shoulders slump just a little. She's discouraged, but not defeated.

"Well, you know if you ever need a travel buddy, all you have to do is ask," she says.

"Thanks, Em. I appreciate it," Zach says. "Is it our turn?"

Game night winds down shortly thereafter. It's just as well. We have a very busy day tomorrow, weather permitting. First, Brittany has blocked off the entire morning in order to show Emma around the city. Thankfully, I don't believe my presence is required for that particular tour. Then, we have a Christmas luncheon for members of the extended royal family. Finally, the wedding rehearsal is scheduled for tomorrow afternoon, followed by another cocktail reception and dinner.

Honestly, sixty percent of being royal is eating with people you barely know in evening gowns that barely fit.

"I still can't believe this is really happening," Emma sighs as we all prepare to take our leave. "I'm going to sleep in a real fairy tale castle and my best friend is really going to marry a real Prince Charming."

"And live happily ever after," Nicolás adds with a sweet smile.

"It's all just so romantic!" Emma exclaims. "Don't you think so, Zach?"

Zach responds by glancing in my direction.

"Yeah," he says. "I do."

And suddenly, I am feeling very warm and light-headed.

That's when Emma clears her throat.

"You know... I'm not sure I remember where my room is. Would you maybe walk with me so I don't get lost?" she asks Zach.

"Actually, I think Britt's suite is closer to your room than mine is. She'll walk with you." Zach tells her. "Right, Britt?"

"Absolutely!" Brittany says. "Come on, Em. Goodnight, everyone!"

"Goodnight, my love," Nicolás bids her. "Sleep well, Emma."

"I'm going to say goodnight as well," I announce, taking the opportunity to slip out before anyone, specifically Lord Weston, offers to escort me back to my room. Besides, my heart is still singing after the moment that Zach and I just shared. I'd like to make my escape before anyone or anything has the chance to ruin it.

Snow is still steadily falling when I finally turn out my light and climb into bed. I nestle beneath the thick sheets and blankets and listen to the gusts of winter wind outside my window. It may seem strange, but I find the sound soothing, perhaps because it reminds me of the coastal breezes back home.

I wonder if Zach will ever see Mondovia... I muse as I lay in the darkness, waiting for sleep to visit me. If he does, it should be in the summertime. That's when the waters are a deep mix of turquoise and cerulean and the air smells like fresh flowers. I picture us walking hand-in-hand along the beach while the crystal-clear Adriatic Sea washes over our feet.

I've just begun to drift off when a gentle knock at the door startles me awake.

"Sophie?" I whisper. But she's in her room, more than likely asleep.

Wrapping myself in my dressing gown, I slip out of bed, switch on the lights, and tiptoe to the door.

"Who is it?" I ask.

"It's me."

Zach.

I open the door to find him still in his day clothes.

"Hey," he greets me, shoving his hands into the pockets of his jeans. "I'm sorry. I woke you up, didn't I?"

"It's all right. I was barely asleep," I tell him. "What's going on? Are you all right?"

"Yeah. I just... I wanted to apologize for this evening. You know, with Emma and everything. And I would have texted you only... I don't have your phone number." That's right. He doesn't. Even after all the time we've spent together.

"We'll have to remedy that," I grin. "And please, you don't need to apologize for Emma. I know the two of you share a lot of memories."

"We do," he admits. "But I'm not sure now is the time to revisit them. Especially when..."

"Especially when what?" I prompt.

He opens his mouth like he's going to say something, but then he immediately closes it again. It's difficult to see in such low lighting, but I think he's blushing.

"I know we haven't known each other that long... and I know the odds are stacked against us..."

"But...?"

He hesitates again. Then, to my surprise, he gives a rather nervous laugh.

105

"It's funny, we've spent so much time together and I've told you so much... but... it's just now hitting me that you're a Princess. And I'm..."

"Completely wonderful?" I supply.

He smiles, looking at once overjoyed and relieved.

"Rose, I don't want Christmas Day to be the last time I see you."

"I don't either," I whisper.

The next thing I know, I'm wrapped up in his strong embrace and he's kissing me like he did the first day we met, on the corner of the city street while snowflakes danced around us. And I'm kissing him back and everything is perfect. Because his warmth, his touch, his kiss is Heaven.

No, it's more than Heaven. When I'm kissing him, no matter where I am, I feel like I'm home. And that is something I've never felt before. Not with anyone. But I feel it with him.

And I think he feels it, too.

Slowly, reluctantly, he releases me and I open my eyes to a whole new world; a world filled with hope and promise. And love.

"I should probably let you get back to sleep," he murmurs, pressing his forehead to mine.

I don't want to let him go. I want him to stay with me. But I know it's impossible.

So I kiss him once more before telling him, "Goodnight." Then, in a rather uncharacteristic moment of silliness, I add, "Parting is such sweet sorrow."

Zach raises an eyebrow before bursting into a fit of laughter.

"Did you just quote Shakespeare?"

"Yes, as a matter of fact," I giggle. *"Romeo and Juliet."*

"Well, as long as our story doesn't end like theirs..."

"Don't worry. It won't," I assure him.

"Good." Then, he kisses me swiftly one last time. "Goodnight, dear Rose who, by any other name, would smell just as sweet."

Oh, God, that was so cheesy. Why did I ever bring Shakespeare into this?

"That's it. That was too much." I laugh. "Begone now."

"I'm sorry," he grins. "Goodnight, Rose."

"Goodnight."

CHAPTER FOURTEEN

Santa Catalina at Christmastime is truly a sight to behold.

Just inside it's grand, ancient doors, a dazzling Christmas tree, glowing with brilliant purple and white lights, stands to greet all who enter the sacred building. Beyond the evergreen, bouquets of red, white, and pink poinsettias surround the fountain of holy water set in the entrance of the nave, which, itself is decorated with glorious strands of garland and dozens of white candles.

I've attended several services here throughout the years, but never at Christmas.

"*Bienvenidos*, Your Royal Highnesses and honoured guests," the priest, Padre Miguel, welcomes us with open arms. "What a pleasure it is to see you all."

"The pleasure is ours, Padre," Princess Isabel tells him.

"I see you've brought quite the party with you."

Unlike the brides and grooms of Britain's royal family, Nicolás and Brittany will not be accompanied by bridesmaids or page boys. In San Cecilian weddings, the parents walk with their sons and daughters down the aisle and then, once the ceremony is done, bear witness to the signing of the marriage certificate. As is so with many aspects of their culture, weddings in San Cecilio are very family-oriented.

They're also rather, for want of a better word, lengthy. That means that those of us who aren't active participants - Lord Weston, Emma, Zach, and I

- are bound to sit in silence for an extended period while Padre Miguel walks Nicolás, Brittany, as well as their parents and other members of the clergy through the service. And God love the good Father, but he does know how to take his time.

We've only been here for fifteen minutes when Zach passes me the first note. Except it's not a note at all. It's a drawing of... something. An animal of some sort.

"Is this a bear?" I hiss.

He shakes his head and then leans over and writes something.

Sloth.

Then he draws something else. A creature with a long neck.

Ah, okay. I know this one.

Giraffe.

Correct. Your turn.

Oh, dear. He's setting me up for failure, isn't he? Then again, he's not a particularly gifted artist either. So I pick up the pencil and give it my best effort.

He takes one look at my creation and scribbles out his guess.

Hippo?

Hippo?! In what universe does that look like a hippo?

No! It's a horse!

Close enough.

That's not even remotely close!

Sure it is. Hippos are "river horses," after all.

I cast a playful sneer in his direction. It's all either of us can do not to laugh.

If I had a Fairy Godmother, my only wish this evening would be for the time to take a nap before tonight's reception and rehearsal dinner. Actually, it would be delightful not to have to attend at all. But I will admit I'm rather looking forward to seeing Zach in his tuxedo again.

"So, how was the rehearsal?" Sophie asks, helping me fasten my midnight blue evening gown.

"Long," I answer honestly. "I should have taken a book."

"Well, I know His Royal Highness and Miss Walker appreciate your presence."

"I suppose. I didn't really do anything. Zach and I mostly entertained ourselves by drawing silly pictures on scrap pieces of paper."

"Oh, really?" Sophie teases.

"Stop it. It's not like that." Actually, it's *exactly* like that.

"You know, he is *very* handsome."

"Yes, I've noticed."

"He's a doctor, too."

"A veterinarian."

"He loves animals. That means he's got a good heart."

"He also has a wonderful sense of humor," I add with a wistful sigh.

And then we both succumb to a fit of girlish giggles.

Once we've recovered, Sophie fetches my tiara and positions it perfectly atop my head.

"Thank you, Sophie," I tell her.

"You look lovely, Your Highness," she replies.

I steady myself and hold my head high as I emerge, once again, from my bedroom and make my way down to the gold drawing room. This time, however, Zach is the one waiting for me on the stairs.

"Oh... wow..." he breathes when he sees me.

I smile, my eyes never leaving his face as I make my descent. When I reach him on the ground floor, he gazes at me for just a moment before taking my hand and bowing.

"You... are beautiful," he says, raising my hand to his lips.

"And you are a dream come true," I tell him. Then, for reasons I can't even begin to understand, I ask, "You're not really thinking of shaving your beard, are you?"

"What?" he laughs. "Where did that come from?"

"When you kissed my hand, I remembered Brittany saying that she wished you'd shave it for the wedding."

"Well, as far as I'm concerned, the only woman allowed to order me to shave my beard is you," he says.

"Oh, good. I like to hear that," I grin.

"Hello." A new voice chimes in.

He and I both turn to see Emma gliding toward us. I hate to say it, but she looks exceptionally gorgeous in an elegant gold dress that doesn't quite qualify as an evening gown but is stunning nevertheless.

"Wow, Em. You look amazing," Zach tells her.

"Thank you," she smiles at him before turning icy eyes on me. "Good evening, Princess Rosalind."

"Good evening to you, Miss Wilson."

"Do you think I could steal Zach for just like, two seconds?" she asks. "I need to talk to him about something. And it's sort of personal."

"Of course," I answer.

"Great," she says.

Then, looping her arm through his, she guides him away from me, across the foyer, and down a darkened corridor. I like to think I have every intention of respecting their privacy, but as soon as I turn to leave, I hear her hushed voice echoing through the castle halls.

"Are you kidding me?" she demands. "You and *Rosalind*?"

"Em, please, don't get upset - "

"How can I *not* be upset? Do you have any idea who she is? She's the one who tried to come between Britt and Nicolás!"

"It wasn't like that - "

"She was supposed to marry your sister's fiancé! She *wanted* to marry him! And now here you are, falling at her feet like a lovestruck teenager... passing notes with her in the middle of Britt's wedding rehearsal..."

"Em, listen to me. She's not the person the media makes her out to be - "

"And that's another thing!" Emma interrupts. "*You* dumped *me* because you didn't want to see your life in the headlines. Newsflash, Romeo! If you date a Princess, your life is going to be nothing *but* headlines!"

"That's not why we broke up, Em."

"Oh, please, spare me the lecture. I was trying to *help* you. To help us! But you made it very clear that you didn't want anything to do with this world - oh, how did you put it? - this world of 'empty titles and meaningless ceremonies?'"

"Emma, I was angry. I said a lot of things that I didn't mean."

"Yeah, that you don't mean *now*. Now that you have an actual Princess swooning over you. Have you even stopped to consider why that is?"

"Why what is?" Zach asks.

"Why she's so interested in you. She's a *Princess*, Zach. She's rich, she's powerful... she could have *anyone*. So why is she wasting her time with a guy like you?"

Her question is succeeded by a heavy silence, and for a moment, I'm afraid that Zach may have taken her words to heart. Then, finally, he speaks. And the words he says make my spirit soar.

"You don't know her."

"I don't have to," Emma argues. "I can see what she's doing. She's using you, Zach. And I'm sorry, I can't just stand by and watch it happen. I love you too much to see you get hurt."

"You know, the reception's probably started by now," Zach announces. "We should head back."

"Zach?" Emma makes one final attempt to hold onto him. "I mean it. I love you. You know I do."

"I believe you," he tells her. "Come on. Let's go."

And that is my cue to leave.

Sprinting all the way to the gold drawing room is no easy feat, especially in heels and an evening gown. Thankfully, I arrive just in time to catch my breath before Zach appears wearing a neutral expression on his handsome face.

"Hey," he smiles at me.

"Hi. Is everything all right?" I ask.

"Oh, yeah. It's fine," he answers. "She just had a few questions about the wedding."

"And about us?"

"Yeah," he sighs.

"She's not happy, is she?"

"She'll be okay," he assures me. "Once she sees Britt and Nicolás, she'll remember why we're all here tonight."

I nod, hoping with all my heart that he's right.

CHAPTER FIFTEEN

It's Christmas Eve and anticipation is in the air. Anticipation for my family to arrive, for the Parade of Stars tonight, and for the royal wedding tomorrow. I've only just opened my eyes and already, I can tell it's going to be a joyous morning.

I'm delighted to report that last night's reception and dinner went off without a single hitch. Brittany and Nicolás were positively radiant, guests were all smiles, and Emma and even Lord Weston were on their best behaviour. Then, after it was all over, Zach escorted me back to my room. And he kissed me. Again. And again. And again.

Then, he said, "You know, I know I don't have a whole lot to offer you. My apartment isn't much of a palace and my car's side-view mirror may or may not be duct-taped to the door..." I couldn't help it. I giggled. "But if you ever want to come visit me in Ohio, I can absolutely take you behind the scenes at the zoo. I can introduce you to the elephants, the giraffes, the flamingos... Now, I can't promise that the flamingos will curtsy, because they're not very smart - "

But I cut him off with a kiss before he had the chance to finish.

"That sounds perfect," I told him.

Now, seven hours later, I'm lying in bed, reliving the moment over and over as the winter sun streams in through my window.

Perfect. Perfect. Everything is perfect.

Then the door to my bedroom opens and Sophie appears.

"Your Highness?" she calls softly. But her voice sounds... off. Like she's nervous or perhaps upset.

"Sophie?" I sit up to face her. "What is it?"

"Your Highness, I'm so sorry, but... I think you should see this," she says, handing me her phone. It's opened to a news article.

Princess Playgirl? Rosalind Romances Not One But TWO New Suitors!

With her former betrothed merely a day away from his wedding to American sweetheart Brittany Walker, Princess Rosalind of Mondovia is setting out to break a few hearts of her own.

Our sources in San Cecilio confirm that throughout her stay at the castle, the Princess has enjoyed a brief fling with Viscount Weston Bentley, a friend of Prince Nicolás and Miss Walker. The young nobleman, who hails from London, is reported to have been quite taken with the Princess and expressed shock and disappointment upon discovering he was not the only man in the young royal's life.

"He was completely blindsided," a source close to the Viscount claims. "Despite not having known her for very long, he was hopeful that their relationship might evolve into something more serious."

And perhaps it may have... had Zachary Walker not arrived on the scene.

That's right. Zachary Walker. Remember him? Brittany's dreamboat of an older brother? Well, it turns out not even Princesses are immune to those blue eyes or magnificent biceps.

"Rosalind was smitten," a friend of the royal family states. "She began pursuing him almost immediately. It didn't matter to her that he was Brittany's

brother or that she was hurting Weston in the process. She just saw Zach and she wanted him."

By now, my stomach has twisted itself into a thousand knots and my extremities are as cold as ice. I don't have to wonder how my personal affairs found their way to the headlines or why they've been so greatly exaggerated. To be frank, I don't even care. I'm just done.

"I can't," I say, handing the phone back to Sophie. "I'm sorry, I can't finish that."

"With all due respect, Your Highness, you need to keep reading," Sophie tells me.

"Why?"

Sophie scrolls down the page until she reaches the last few paragraphs. Then she passes the phone back to me.

All of this breaks amidst reports that her brother, Crown Prince Robert, plans to renounce his title, relinquishing his status as heir apparent... and making Rosalind next in line for the throne of Mondovia. While the Palace has yet to make an official statement, speculations are already swirling throughout the Kingdom as to how the promiscuous Princess will adapt to her new responsibilities as heir and her new role as future Queen.

Future Queen.

Heart racing, hands trembling, I drop the phone onto the bed as though it's burned me.

"No. No, this isn't right," I say.

"You didn't know?"

"No, because it isn't true."

"How can you be sure?"

"Because it isn't. My parents would have said something. *Robert* would have said something. If he had been planning it, or even *considering* it, I would have known. For Heaven's sake, this isn't exactly a decision one makes overnight."

"But what if it is true?" Sophie asks.

"It isn't. It can't be." And to prove it, I reach for my own phone and press the **Call** button next to my brother's name. If anyone can clear this up once and for all, he can.

Unfortunately, my call takes me straight to his voicemail.

"Blast," I mutter under my breath. He and my mother are flying in today. They're probably already on the plane. "Okay. All right. Here's what's going to happen. As far as you and I are concerned, this... this *rubbish* was never published. We're not going to bring it up. We're not even going to think about it. If someone happens to bring it up, which I pray they do not, we tell them that it's just another media-conceived scandal meant to entice readers the day before the wedding."

Sophie nods in agreement.

Once I've dressed and brushed my teeth, I summon up every ounce of strength and self-assurance I've ever possessed and make my way down to breakfast.

Perhaps I'm overreacting. There is a chance that this won't be so bad. In fact, there's a chance that it will be nothing at all. It's possible that no one has even seen the article and that I'm getting myself worked up over nothing.

It's fine, I assure myself, opening the door to the dining hall. *Everything is going to be fine.*

I've no sooner shown my face, however, than the room falls completely silent.

Or not.

Brittany is the first to greet me.

"Good morning, Rose!"

"Good morning to you, too," I reply.

I glance around the table for Zach's face. He's there, sitting between Nicolás and Emma. He smiles at me, but his eyes are anxious, uncertain. What I wouldn't give for just a moment alone with him.

"Rosalind, please, come join us," Nicolás bids me.

I nod and take my place at the table next to Lord Weston. For a single blessed moment, I truly believe we'll be able to enjoy our meal in peace.

Then, of course, *she* speaks.

"So, is it true?" Emma wants to know.

"Really, Em?" Zach scolds.

"What? Someone had to ask," Emma defends herself. Then she turns her attention back to me. "Is your brother really giving up the throne?"

"No," I answer with certainty.

"Are you sure?"

"Very. It's a fabrication of the press. And quite possibly their most outlandish one yet."

"But they weren't wrong about everything," Emma notes. "I mean, what about you and Zach?"

Oh God, not now. *Please* not now.

"What about them?" Brittany asks.

"You know, I really don't think now's the time," Zach says.

"I agree," I say.

"Wait, *is* there something going on?" Nicolás asks.

"You could say that," Weston remarks.

"What? Since when?" Brittany asks, her wide blue eyes flitting from me to Zach and back to me.

"Since we got to know one another," Zach answers.

"Why didn't you tell us?" Brittany demands.

"Because we were still trying to figure things out ourselves."

"And because we knew we'd be facing an inquiry," I remark.

"Sorry. I know I'm asking a lot of questions. I'm just trying to process it," Brittany explains.

"Well, listen, the last thing I want - that we want - is to cause a stir the day before your wedding. Which is why the release of that wretched article couldn't have come at a less convenient time," I add with a frigid glare in Emma's direction.

"Forget the article," Nicolás tells me. "I say that if the two of you are happy, then we're happy."

"I'm still in shock!" Brittany laughs. "I just can't believe I didn't know."

"You've been preoccupied," Zach reminds her.

"So that's it then? Everyone is just *okay* with this?" Emma asks. "They've been sneaking around behind your back for over a week."

"That's nothing. Britt and I dated for two *months* before we told anyone," Nicolás says.

"And you didn't tell *me* until you were already engaged," I quip.

"Yeah... Sorry about that," Nicolás grimaces.

"Don't worry," I tell him. "All is forgiven."

After breakfast, my wish for a moment alone with Zach is granted. We decide to step outside for a breath of fresh winter air and a walk through the snow-blanketed gardens.

"So, that wasn't exactly the way I would have preferred everyone to find out," Zach remarks with a wry grin.

"No, not at all," I agree. "But at least it's out in the open now."

"Are you... okay with it being out in the open?"

"Yes. That is I'm okay with our family and friends knowing. I'll admit I'm not thrilled by the idea of our relationship being broadcast to the public on social media."

"Me neither," Zach agrees. "So, what do we do?"

"I suppose we take it one day at a time," I answer. "Unfortunately, as a member of the royal family, I'm not permitted to speak out or address the media when they print stories about me. No matter how inaccurate."

"That's got to be rough."

"Some days more than others. But I'm learning to accept that it's a part of life. A part of *this* life, anyway." I don't want anything I say to discourage Zach from being with me, but I also know that he deserves to know what he's getting into. Although, after having watched Brittany transition from girl-next-door to royal, he may already have a pretty good idea of what awaits him.

That is, if he were to choose it. If we stay together.

"And um... what about the other thing?" he asks.

I don't have to wonder what he means.

"It isn't true. My brother would never give up his claim."

"What if he did?"

There it is. The question I never wanted to consider. The question I shouldn't *have* to consider. Robert will be King of Mondovia one day and I shall gladly stand by him as his sister and subject. Any other scenario is inconceivable.

"I don't know," I answer honestly. "Back when I was betrothed to Nicolás, I rather liked the idea of being married to a sovereign. But there's a distinct difference between Princess Consort and Queen Regent. Of course, I like to think that I would accept the responsibility with grace and courage... but Zach, I think that I'd be terrified. I mean, that kind of decision... it would change my entire life."

"Yeah, it would," he says, lacing his fingers through mine. "But you know, that's not necessarily a bad thing." I glance up to see absolute sincerity in his beautiful eyes. "Who knows? Maybe it's your destiny."

"My destiny?" I smirk.

"What? You don't believe in destiny?"

My immediate answer to that question is no, I don't believe in destiny. A supernatural force that guides the pattern of our lives is something for the storybooks. But then... what were the chances that Nicolás and Brittany would meet? Probably about the same as the chances that I would literally run into Zach at a bookstore... mere hours before we would be formally introduced.

Finally, I know what to say.

"I didn't think I did. Until I met you."

And to prove it, I wrap my arms around his shoulders and press my mouth to his. He returns my kiss wholeheartedly, and even though we're still hours away from *El Desfile de Estrellas,* I'm already seeing stars.

We linger in the garden for a few moments longer, kissing, laughing, and then kissing again, before a gust of winter wind nearly sweeps both of us off of our feet. I'm so startled that I actually shriek.

"We should probably head back inside," Zach suggests, trying and failing to conceal his amusement.

"I agree," I shiver. Then I turn, fully prepared to sprint back to the castle, when Zach reaches out for my hand.

"Hey," he says. "For what it's worth, I think you'd make an amazing Queen."

CHAPTER SIXTEEN

When my mother and brother arrive at the castle, I'm waiting on the stairs to welcome them. I knew that I would be delighted to see them, but I didn't realize just how much I missed them until I've thrown myself into my brother's arms.

"I'm so sorry I missed your call. I was on a plane," he tells me.

"I know," I laugh.

"Oh, Rosalind, just look at you," my mother sighs. "You look wonderful."

"Thank you, Mum," I smile.

"Mathilde!" Princess Isabel's voice rings throughout the foyer.

"My dearest Isabel!" My mother's face lights up as she embraces her friend.

"It has been too long," Isabel says.

"Much too long," my mother agrees.

"Something tells me she's more excited about seeing Isabel than seeing me," I mutter to Robert.

"Something tells me you're right," he grins.

"We'll leave them to it, then," I tell him. "Come with me. I have someone I'd like you to meet."

I lead him into the sitting room, where I last saw Zach, Nicolás, and Brittany enjoying a few moments of peace and quiet before tonight's festivities. When we arrive, I find that Emma has joined them as well, though she doesn't look at all happy to be there. Her shoulders are slumped and she's positioned herself as far away from Zach as possible. Her demeanor brightens considerably, however, the moment she sets eyes on my brother.

"Robert!" Nicolás exclaims, rising to greet him. "Good to see you!"

"Good to see you, too," Robert echoes his sentiments. "I believe congratulations are in order."

"Thank you, thank you," Nicolás beams. "Please, come in! Meet my bride! Brittany, love..."

At his beckoning, Brittany leaps up off of the sofa and bounds over to where we're standing.

"Hi! I'm Brittany. It is so nice to meet you," she smiles, shaking his hand and curtsying at the same time.

"You've never curtsied to me," I tease her.

"I'm sorry!" she laughs. "Do you want me to?"

"It's fine."

"Seems like the two of you have become pretty good friends," Robert comments. "You should know, Miss Walker, that Rosalind has told me nothing but good things about you."

"Really? Oh, my God, Rose..." She almost sounds like she's about to cry as she wraps her arms around me.

"Rose?" Robert asks. "I thought that was my nickname for you."

"It sort of caught on here, too," I explain. "Mostly thanks to Zach."

Zach takes that as his cue to join us.

"Hi. Zachary Walker," he introduces himself. "It's an honour to make your acquaintance, Your Highness."

He sounds so proper that I almost giggle. I suppose he's hoping to make a good impression.

"Are you the veterinarian, then?" Robert asks.

Oh, God.

He knows.

He must have read that article! Or one of the dozens it surely spawned.

"Yep. That'd be me," Zach answers with a nervous grin.

"Robert, be nice," I warn him.

"What? I'm always nice."

"Right."

Suddenly, Emma erupts with laughter and strolls over to join us.

"Rosalind, what are you talking about? He seems *very* nice," she fawns in a voice as sweet as syrup. "Hi, I'm Emma Wilson. I'm Britt's best friend."

"Nice to meet you. Robert." As if my brother needed to introduce himself.

"You know, it's funny, I was just telling Britt and Nicolás how much I would love to visit Macedonia."

"Oh, really? And why is that?" Robert asks, like a jerk.

"Well, I mean, it just has to be a pretty amazing place with you as Prince."

"Em," Brittany hisses. "Em, it's Mondovia."

"What?"

"Robert and Rosalind are from *Mondovia*, not Macedonia."

"Oh, my God!" Emma exclaims, blushing a brilliant crimson. "Oh, of course that's what I meant. I'm *so* sorry, Your Highness."

"Don't apologize. It's a common mistake," Robert assures her. "You wouldn't believe how many tourists wind up in Mondovia by accident."

While Emma, Brittany, and Nicolás all have a laugh, Zach takes my hand and says, "Your brother seems cool."

"Eh, he's all right."

Of course, the truth is I adore my brother and I'm so very happy to see him. We've yet to address those *other* rumours, but for the moment, I don't care. All that matters is that he's here, we're all together, and because of that, it's finally beginning to feel like Christmas.

The night sky is clear and alive with the light of a million stars as we gather along the street leading to Santa Catalina. Each onlooker bears a single white candle, creating a pathway of light for *El Desfile de Estrellas.* It's a sacred and serene setting and despite the bitter chill in the air, I feel the most divine warmth. Warmth and joy and love.

As the procession of stars approaches, I find myself scanning the multitude of magnificent creations for our own works of art. I spot the family who received Nicolás's star almost immediately. And then the nurse who received Brittany's. The university student who selected my star carries it with the utmost pride and respect. But it's the little boy who inherited Zach's Death Star who steals every heart under the dark Valoña sky.

It really was a wonderful idea, making those stars. The more I observe, the easier it is to see how much love and hope and wonder are reflected in the eyes of those who bear them. And of those who bear witness. It's a glorious sight, all those many, many stars of every size and every colour.

After the last star passes, we follow the parade into Santa Catalina for Midnight Mass as the bells of the Cathedral's carillon ring out into the night.

By the time we return to the castle, it's nearly two in the morning. I know I should be feeling exhausted, but the truth is I'm wide awake. Sadly, the same cannot be said for my companions.

"I would love to stay up and wait for Santa with you, but I am wiped out," Zach tells me, stifling a huge yawn.

"Actually, we don't have Santa here," Nicolás informs him, also looking very sleepy. "We exchange gifts on *El Día de los Reyes Magos.* Three Kings Day."

"Oh, okay. So Santa's not coming anyway," Zach comments. "In that case, I'm going to bed." He kisses me swiftly on the forehead, then the mouth, before bidding all of us a final goodnight. Nicolás and Brittany follow shortly thereafter.

"I suppose we should get some rest, too," I tell Robert, who, strangely enough, doesn't seem the least bit worn out, even after his day of international travel.

"Actually, Rose... there's something I'd like to discuss with you. If that's all right. I know you've had a long day."

"Of course," I tell him. "What is it?"

"Maybe we should go somewhere a little more private."

I agree and lead him into the sitting room, which is sure to be empty this time of night. I immediately take a seat on the sofa and wait for him to join me. But he doesn't. Instead, he plants his feet firmly in front of me and fidgets with his golden ring.

"Robert?" I prod him gently.

Finally, he takes a deep breath and begins.

"I'm all but certain you've read the reports by now."

Ah, yes. *Those* reports.

"I have," I confirm. "But you don't have to explain them to me. I know how often the media likes to embellish."

"Indeed," Robert chuckles.

"I just don't understand why they'd print something that is so blatantly false. I mean, it's one thing to run a little white lie or an over-exaggeration, but to concoct something that has the potential to - "

"The thing is, it's not false," Robert speaks all in a rush. So rushed, in fact, that I can't have heard him correctly.

"What?" I ask, my heart beating wildly against my chest.

"Rose, I - I don't want to be King."

I sit in silence for several moments, trying to process what he's telling me.

"I don't understand," I breathe.

Robert sighs and takes a seat next to me.

"I've had my doubts for a while now," he explains. "At first, I wrote off my concerns as uncertainty, fear of responsibility. But the harder I tried to push myself past those thoughts, the more they began to consume me."

"Robert, I... I never knew."

"I didn't want you to know. I didn't want *anyone* to know."

"So why now? What's changed?"

"You," he answers simply. "Or rather, your circumstances. Before, you were bound to Nicolás and to the throne of San Cecilio. I couldn't ask you to give up your future, especially when you seemed so delighted by the prospect of it. But then - "

"Then Nicolás broke off our betrothal," I answer for him.

"And that's when I began to really consider it."

"And yet, you still didn't say anything."

"I couldn't. You were so distraught at the time. I didn't want to burden you with my reservations."

"Even though those reservations concerned my future?"

"I don't have to do this, Rose," he tells me, taking my hand. "The crown is my responsibility, not yours. But I can't help but feel that, as a leader, as a sovereign, you make so much more sense than I do."

"How can you say that?"

"Because it's true. You were made for this life. You hold in esteem the traditions and formalities... I daresay you even enjoy them. You were fully prepared to take on the role of sovereign here in San Cecilio, without question."

"Yes, but becoming a monarch is so much more than a respect for tradition or the willingness to jump in with both feet."

"And you understand that, which is more than I can say for a few of the world's leaders out there." That actually gets a smile out of me. "Listen, we don't have to decide anything tonight. It is Christmas Eve, after all. I just wanted you to know the truth. And to think about it."

My mind is racing with a million reasons why I should refuse.

I'm not bold enough.

I'm not smart enough.

The crown is his birthright.

The country adores him.

And yet, in spite of all of these doubts and fears, I hear myself whisper, "I will."

Robert smiles, his hazel eyes aglow.

"I love you, Rose," he tells me.

"I love you, too."

CHAPTER SEVENTEEN

It all ends, as so many stories do, with happily ever after.

The ceremony is everything a royal wedding should be and more. Brittany and her father arrive at Santa Catalina in a fancy vintage car that I can't name, but it renders both Zach and Robert weak at the knees. I'll never understand what it is with men and cars. Besides, Brittany looks far more beautiful than any old automobile.

Her ball gown style wedding dress is stunning, covered with lace and adorned with tiny crystals. It's a little more extravagant than any gown I would choose for myself, but it looks spectacular on her. Her veil is a simple, modest one, held in place by a glittering diamond and sapphire tiara I recognize from the many times I've seen Princess Isabel wear it. That tiara has always been one of my favourites, one I had once hoped to inherit. But seeing it now, I realize it was made for Brittany.

Just like Nicolás, whose eyes glisten with tears of joy and love as he watches his bride walk down the aisle. I've never seen him smile so brightly as he does when Brittany finally joins him at the altar.

"*I love you*," he whispers to her.

The service itself is rather long, as is to be expected of a royal wedding mass. More than once, I catch myself drifting into a daydream. But I always return, for I don't want to miss a moment.

Finally, Padre Miguel asks us all to rise.

"Dear friends, let us pray to the Lord to bless this union. Father, look with love upon thy servants, Nicolás and Brittany, guide them in their marriage, and bless them in all their days to come. We ask this in the name of the Father, and of the Son, and of the Holy Spirit."

"Amen."

"Finally, by the power vested in me, I now pronounce you husband and wife. Your Royal Highness, you may kiss your bride."

And so he does.

"Ladies and gentlemen," Padre Miguel continues. "It is my honour to present to you Their Royal Highnesses, Prince Nicolás and Princess Brittany of San Cecilio."

While Nicolás and Brittany enjoy an open carriage ride throughout the streets of Valoña, the rest of us are escorted back to the castle to relax and change for the reception. Well, *I* get to change for the reception. Zach and his family have to wait until after they've posed with the bride and groom for the official wedding portraits.

For my final night in San Cecilio, I select my favourite emerald green ball gown. I'm not exactly sure what to expect this evening, but Brittany insisted that we come prepared to "dance the night away."

I'm in the process of slipping my shoes on when my phone lights up.

One New Message: Zach
Finally done with pictures! Where are you?

Grinning from ear to ear, I type out a response.

My room. I've nearly finished changing.

When you're ready, would you meet me in the library?

Of course.

Eager to enjoy a few moments alone with him before this evening's frenzy, I scamper down to the library as quickly as I can in my admittedly restrictive ball gown. He's already there, waiting for me.

"God, every time, I think you can't get more beautiful," he says. "And then you go and prove me wrong."

"Oh, I do apologize," I smile.

"I think I can forgive you," he winks. "So, they really did it, didn't they? They really got married. My sister really is a Princess."

"She is."

"That's weird."

"You've kissed a Princess."

"That's weird, too. Then again, Han Solo *also* kissed a Princess and - wait. Wait a minute. Oh my God."

"What?" I ask, suddenly quite concerned.

"Han Solo kissed a Princess. And *I* kissed a Princess! Do you know what that means?"

"That you're both absurdly lucky?"

"It means that *I'm* like Han Solo! Oh man, this is the best day of my life. I need to tell someone. I need everyone to know that I am Han Solo."

Oh my God, what have I done?

"So, this it what our relationship has come to, is it?"

134

"Hey, you should feel like the luckiest girl in the galaxy. You get to date Han Solo."

"That's it. I'm done," I laugh.

"I'm sorry, I'm sorry. I'll stop," he promises. "Believe it or not, this isn't actually why I asked you to meet me." Then, he reaches up to one of the shelves and grabs a rather poorly wrapped parcel. "This is."

"What is it?"

"Your Christmas present," he answers. "I'm sorry it's wrapped in tissue paper. I didn't really have a whole lot to work with."

"But... I didn't get you anything."

"That's okay. I'll let you make it up to me later," he teases as he hands me the package.

Carefully, I unwrap the paper to find an old and very well-loved copy of *The Giver*.

"Zach..."

"I know you've already read it, but this is the copy that's gone everywhere with me since the eighth grade."

"And... you want to give it to me? What if something happens to it?"

"I trust you," he smiles. "Besides, I'm kind of hoping that I'll be seeing you again sooner rather than later. That way, you know, I can check up on it. See how it's doing."

Again, I laugh, but this time, my laughter is tinged with tears.

"I think this is the best present I've ever received," I tell him. "Thank you."

"You're welcome," he smiles.

Then, he takes me in his arms and lowers his mouth to mine. He hasn't kissed me like this since that night in the hall and I'm not ashamed to admit I don't know how I'll do without him kissing me until I see him again.

But I'm not going to dwell on that now, because we still have tonight. And I can't help but feel that it's going to be nothing short of magical.

As it turns out, I was mistaken.

Not about the evening being magical. It has been, in every possible way, from the seven sparkling Christmas trees to the monumental wedding cake to the look on Nicolás's face every time he sees his bride in her elegant white party dress.

No, I was wrong about the dancing.

We are, in fact, dancing the night away, but not the way I had been anticipating. I came expecting to waltz to a delightful, classy string ensemble. What Princess Brittany has supplied, however... is a disc jockey.

"Come on, Rose, really?" Robert laughs when I express my surprise. "I'm older than you are and even I knew there was going to be a DJ!"

"But I don't know how to dance to this music!"

"Oh, for God's sake," Robert rolls his eyes. "Zach! Come teach your girlfriend how to dance."

"It would be my pleasure, Your Highness," Zach grins. Then, with a rather mischievous gleam in his eye, he takes my hand and leads me out onto the dance floor. "You're going to want to hold on to your tiara!" he warns me as he begins to move with no real rhyme nor reason.

I try my best to mimic his motions but I'm afraid I look rather silly. I certainly feel silly.

"This is so hard!" I laugh.

"Nah, it's easy. Listen, just let your body do what it wants to. Don't over think it. Move with the music and have fun."

And so I do. Or at least, I try. And do you know something? It *is* fun. The music is loud and upbeat and far more invigorating than a classical composition played on the violin. Even Lord Weston and Emma seem to be enjoying themselves as they fall into rhythm with one another.

After a while, I lose track of time, faces around me begin to blur, and my inhibitions fade into a swirling storm of music, laughter, and a thousand Christmas lights. I dance with Zach. I dance with my brother. I dance with Brittany. Then I dance with Zach again, falling into his arms, feeling as light and carefree as a snowflake on the wind.

And as I look into his eyes, those gorgeous eyes that shine like blue starlight, I begin to think that perhaps this isn't the end after all.

Perhaps happily ever after is only the beginning.

EPILOGUE

Breaking: Prince Robert of Mondovia Officially Steps Down
King David and Queen Mathilde Name Rosalind New Heir Apparent
Princess Rosalind Has Officially Been Anointed as Mondovia's Next Queen

Six months after she attended the royal wedding of her former betrothed, Princess Rosalind Elisabetta Marie Claremont was formally declared Crown Princess and heir to the throne of Mondovia.

Their Majesties, King David and Queen Mathilde, are said to be very pleased that their daughter will succeed them.

"They're thrilled," an insider confirms. "This past year, and especially in the last six months, they've watched Rosalind mature and grow into a remarkable young woman. They are very, very proud of her."

The Princess was anointed and crowned heir apparent in a ceremony at the palace early Saturday afternoon. In attendance was her long-distance boyfriend, American veterinarian Zachary Walker who, according to reports, is in the process of interviewing for jobs in Mondovia. Present also were Dr. Walker's sister, Princess Brittany and her husband (and Rosalind's former betrothed!), Prince Nicolás of San Cecilio.

Despite initial rumours that the two Princesses do not get along, it appears that they are actually very close. On Friday, they were spotted enjoying lunch together at a local Mondovian cafe, after which, they are reported to have gone shopping.

"They're great friends," a source close to both royals confirms. "Sure, their relationship got off to a bit of

an awkward start, but now they're as close as close can be. They talk constantly and are very supportive of each other."

It's said that Princess Rosalind has been instrumental in helping Brittany adjust to royal life, offering her advice, guidance, and even comfort.

"Who knows?" our source continues. "One day, they may even be sisters."

Could wedding bells indeed be ringing for Princess Rosalind? Royal watchers can only hope!

ACKNOWLEDGEMENTS

Thank you, as always, to my Lord and Savior.

Thank you to my parents for always believing in me.

Thank you to my sister for pushing me to be the best I can be (this is something I definitely need to work on).

Thank you to the Hallmark Channel for the inspiration.

And finally, thank you to my friends and readers. Without you, none of this would be possible.

© 2017 by Fervent Images – Tim Malek

JACQUELINE E. SMITH is the award-winning author of the CEMETERY TOURS series, the BOY BAND series, and TRASHY ROMANCE NOVEL. A longtime lover of words, stories, and characters, Jacqueline earned her Master's Degree in Humanities from the University of Texas at Dallas in 2012. She lives and writes in Dallas, Texas.

Made in the USA
Middletown, DE
07 November 2019

78050155R00087